Also by Ellis Sharp

Novels

The Dump
Unbelievable Things
Walthamstow Central
Intolerable Tongues
To Wetumpka
Lamees Najim
The Orwell Girl
Neglected Writer
What Vronsky Did Next

Short Fiction

Lenin's Trousers
(with Mac Daly) *Engels on Video*
To Wanstonia
Driving My Baby Back Home
Aria Fritta
Quin Again and other stories
Dead Iraqis: Selected Short Stories

Non-Fiction

Sharply Critical

ELLIS SHARP

THE ALEPPO BUTTON

Zoilus Press

First published in Great Britain by Malice Aforethought Press, 1991

Reissued with five additional stories by Zoilus Press, 2021

ISBN 9781999735913

The additional stories in this edition comprise the contents of three chapbooks first published by Malice Aforethought Press in 1988 and 1991. These five stories are "General Jaruzelski's Sunglasses", "The Problem with the President's Mouth", "Dear Blank", "A Quiet Morning for the Pound" and "Giacinta's Clams". The author has also appended additional "Afterthoughts".

Contents

For Frank and Heidi

Here I discovered the true Causes of many great
Events that have surprized the World ...

Lemuel Gulliver, *Travels into several
Remote Nations of the World* (1726)

The Story of Julian Iron

People remember Stalin in different ways. Dissident Soviet bibliophiles used to whisper that his fingers were unexpectedly buttery, and that books returned after a comradely loan would be found to contain page after page stained with blurred grease prints. Then there are the lurid tales put out by historians and journalists (few if any of whom had ever met the man) portraying him as a devious, dubious, paranoid, blood-drenched tyrant. It is true that one or two revolutionary groups have attempted to set things straight by publishing instructive pamphlets attesting to Stalin's astonishing intellect and his keen interest in Marxism, linguistics, calculus, underwater archaeology, chess, palindromic verse, nutrition, ballooning, and biology, but on the whole the picture remains a negative one.

The problem, it seems to me, is that everyone remembers Stalin's Russian period and completely overlooks his later years in England. Consider, for instance, the windswept seaside resort of Bognor Regis. Nowadays if you were to hop out in front of passers-by in the high street and shout "Joseph Stalin!" they would probably mutter, "Communist monster!" or edge nervously away, blank expressions on their plump, flushed faces, as if you were mad. Only one or two would remember that he was once the local M.P., regarded in his time as a first rate constituency worker, whose passionate concern about the erosion of the esplanade did not in any way detract from his interest in local canals, his encouragement of the West Wittering Poet's Circle or his determination to get a better deal for pig farmers.

Stalin has only himself to blame for the uneven contours of his reputation. Fatigued and bored by the strains of high office, it was entirely his own decision to disappear. And what better way of disappearing than to convince the world that you are dead? When I read the story of how poor Lavrenty Beria stood beside the fresh corpse, shouted, "What a marvellous day! We are free!" – and then first one, and then the other eye opened – When I go back and look one more time at the communiqué of the Central Committee ("Comrade Stalin has suffered a cerebral haemorrhage affecting vital areas of the brain") – When I read the medical bulletin – *pulse rate of 108/116 a minute, irregular; the heart is enlarged to a moderate degree* – I seem to see Joseph, devilish fictionalist that he was, crouched in the fading shadows, chuckling quietly to himself. The waxy appearance of the corpse was widely noted.

He needed an accomplice. What a typical master stroke to get chubby, merry-eyed Nikita Kruschev not only to arrange his crossing of the border but also to denounce him at the Twentieth Party Congress. Brilliant! Any lingering doubts which the Soviet people may have had about the reality of their leader's death were finally extinguished. The result is that even today almost everyone in the USSR firmly believes that Stalin died in Moscow in March 1953.

Here in England there is less excuse for such illusions. In 1957 Stalin was a familiar figure on the promenade at Bognor. His portly profile was often to be seen as he took a brisk afternoon stroll past Butlin's holiday camp (its high wire fences stirring who knows what memories of the land he had abandoned). It was not long before he became a popular figure around the town, even something of a "character". Mature ladies in deckchairs, their plump bottoms subjecting the pink and vanilla striped canvas to extraordinary tensions, would spot him in the distance and beckon him impatiently to their sides. Then, sure of a sympathetic response, they would release furious complaints about litter and tourists. Upon sighting Stalin, dogs would likewise experience a strange helplessness in the rear of their bodies and would enthusiastically seek to attract his attention, wagging their tails dementedly. Small boys would run whooping to beg boiled sweets and sherbet lemons, and if you gazed into the misty, rosy distance you would be sure to see fishermen, beaming as they scraped their herring and nodding their old wise grizzled heads in greeting. Stalin was like that: he brought out a comradely feeling of warmth and affection in everyone who met him.

There is even the story of the ladybird which flew from a hedge and landed on Stalin's shoulder. At first the little creature simply wandered the slopes of grey corduroy, bemused by its almost mystical sense of well-being. Then, gazing up at that great chin in the sky, it realized where it was. Holding up its first two legs the ladybird used the now obsolete Paget-Gorman sign language system to communicate to Stalin its delight at encountering him – after which it repeated the message in Morse, deftly manoeuvring a blade of grass across the black spots on its shell. Stalin – it was typical of the man – returned the greetings, firstly by Paget-Gorman, then by tapping on his teeth.

My father was one of the first people to become friendly with the lonely Russian exile. When he first arrived in Bognor Stalin did not go out much. He remained behind a closed door, prone to gloom. In those days he was living in a bedsitter above the Chinese laundry opposite Woolworths. His supply of black market sterling was almost exhausted, and in winter he was reduced to a battered one-bar electric fire for warmth. Stalin set out to improve his English and each day his vocabulary and intellect did battle with the crossword puzzle in the *Daily Express* and two or three pages of *My Early Life* by Winston Churchill.

When, at last, the Russian shyly emerged from his solitude, it was this latter habit which first drew him to my father's attention. Three days in a row my father, strolling home from his solicitor's office near the pier, had observed the shabbily dressed gentleman with the thick moustache immersed in that interesting book. On the fourth day my father could contain himself no longer. He stepped briskly across to the seafront bench where Stalin sat with his back to the wind and squeezed the stranger's plump hand. Though momentarily shocked by the spongy softness of the Russian's flesh, nothing impeded his blurt of blue enthusiasm. "A remarkable story, sir! Remarkable!" Stalin, perplexed by my father's gasps of delight, then gratified, then slightly baffled by the sky-blue mist forming between them, blushed and mumbled something deep, incomprehensible and profound. Then he allowed himself to be persuaded back to our house for a warming glass of port.

"This is Jane," said my father, indicating my sister, who in those days was a flat chested rectangle topped with a porridge-grey face. Jane smiled politely through her silver brace and went back to her magazine.

My father's face darkened. "And that," he added, glancing at the shadowy corner where I squatted, prodding a spider, "is Midge."

Stalin beamed down at me through the cobwebs from a great height. "Hello, Midge," he said. His face seemed to be veiled behind a grey, wiry mesh. He bent down and gave me a sudden, unasked for hug. The pressure of Stalin's embrace sent three or four pockets of stale gas spurting at an implausible velocity from the prison of my body. These abrupt and unexpected explosions caused our guest to jump back, trembling. Old war memories, I suppose. While my father stood crimson faced, frozen, mute, Stalin regained his composure. For seventy-five seconds (I was timing him with my Mickey Mouse stopwatch) the great Russian chewed thoughtfully on a length of cobweb, then spat it out with a scowl. Stalin's cheeks and chin, I saw, were red and pitted with pockmarks. I burst into tears and he at once dissolved into a shimmer of strawberry blotches and raspberry smears.

"He's not used to strangers," my father gruffly explained, glaring at me as he hurried Stalin out of the room.

In truth, my father was ashamed of me. At that time I was only seven years old and my abnormality was not immediately obvious. Not that it had escaped my class at school – hence the nickname. I think my father felt that it was unnatural for the Secretary of the West Bognor Conservative Association to have a midget for his only son. It reflected badly on his virility. It smacked of anarchistic traits roaming wildly through his genes.

I will say this for Stalin. My diminutive stature (I am only just three feet tall) did not bother him at all. In fact I think he rather liked small people. As our friendship blossomed he never once mentioned our first, unfortunate encounter. Indeed, he seemed to have a special regard for little Midge. How well we hit it off! I loved to hear from his own lips the story of his great journey to England; of how he hid in forests and lived off berries; of the birds which he strangled with his own hands. "Develop superhuman qualities, Midge," he used to confide, "and they will always see you through."

Saying this he used to recall how, despite having both arms incapacitated by mildew, he was not deterred from jumping from a liner's white hatch into a black ocean. Aligning the stars against the tip of his nose, he found his way from the Baltic to the North Sea, which (to counteract the threat of *ennui*) he swam on his back, mastering imaginary chess conundrums and using the third and fourth toes of each foot to propel himself at a steady four knots until he reached Lowestoft.

Stalin soon became a regular visitor to our house. He brought me tanks (which were always losing their turrets and their caterpillar tracks) or dumpy little men holding flame throwers. While I smashed the Third Reich and the international Trotskyist conspiracy, the adults talked politics in the room above. Stalin had broken the news of his real identity to my father quite early on. At first my father had been a little perturbed by the unexpected revelation but he soon recognised that the Russian would be quite a catch for the Conservative Party. As J.S. shrewdly pointed out, he himself had personal knowledge of the horrors of Seychellism which ought surely to be brought to the attention of the voters of West Sussex.

I regret to say that not everyone in the West Bognor Conservative Association welcomed the newcomer. It was not so much the natural healthy-minded Conservative mistrust of foreigners, it was more the question of Stalin's past.

At the meeting called at the Conservative Club to discuss the question of whether or not to admit Stalin to Party membership my father strode on to the stage, raised his powerful arms and quelled the mutterings. In those days, before his unhappy collision with the lunar module, he was an impressive figure – six foot six of muscle and scar tissue, with blazing blue eyes and bright black hair. His teeth were as white as the cuttlefish which littered Bognor beach at low tide, his moustache conjured memories of the Battle of Britain, and his nostrils were pear shaped and manly. He spoke in a clipped, metallic voice, like the red weighing machine at the end of the pier.

He quietly explained to the assembly that it was preposterous to believe that one man alone could possibly be responsible for the deaths of seventy million or twenty million or however many million it was supposed to be.

Besides, he cried, Conservatives had always prided themselves on their tolerance – not like the other parties. Could not bygones be bygones? Was it not water under the bridge? My father pointed to J.S., sitting quietly at the back of the room, completely absorbed in a copy of *The Gathering Storm*. "Does he *look* like a mass murderer?" he thundered. All the middle-aged women present shook their heads. "My friends," he continued, "we Conservatives are not, like Seychellists, swayed by empty emotion and sentimentality, are we?" (More shaking of heads and cries of "No!" and "Certainly not!") "My friends, we Conservatives pride ourselves – do we not? – on our realism." (Cries of "Yes!" and "He's right!") "Above all else we know that life is cruel, that some are born to succeed, others to fail. Let me remind you that Sir Winston Churchill himself always had a tremendous respect and admiration for our friend sitting back there. He helped us out in Spain, in Greece, in all *kinds* of places. He has played his part in ridding the world of the scarlet fever of Bolshevism. I might add that our friend is not one of those namby-pamby softies who believes in sparing the rod or the noose. He believes in punishing the criminal –

not in featherbedding him!" (Applause.) "What is more he has many interesting new ideas regarding the development and expansion of our prison service. My friends, I call on Joseph Stalin to say a few words here to you tonight."

There was warm, friendly applause as Stalin, nervously stroking his damp moustache, put down the book and made his way to the front of the room. He began with a few well received remarks about England, its invigorating climate, its proud traditions, Shakespeare, potted jam, kettles, the Brontës, thatch, the Mau Mau menace, Westminster Abbey, the need to protect the interests of the manufacturers of china egg cups with legs on, dog excreta on the esplanade, the unacceptable colour of the pier weighing machine, potted jam, Shakespeare, and the inestimable virtues of the royal family. He compared this to the black nightmare of Seychellism – the long queues outside deserted bakeries, the form-filling and bureaucracy, the seizure of the widow's mite, the bad weather, and the stifling of all free enterprise and personal initiative. He warned against easy answers, the shallow emotive appeals of Seychellists to the redistribution of wealth and other chimaeras. He concluded, his voice trembling, by calling for more soldiers, policemen and prison officers to help put the Great back into Britain again.

The applause was loud and long. Within three years he was the town's Member of Parliament (the previous M.P. having disappeared off the pier one foggy evening). Soon afterwards he married my sister, who by then was no longer a rectangle but a figure eight, with swellings. Now he was no longer "Mr Stalin" but simply "Joe". Before long he had changed his name to Iron. Julian Iron. It was thought best. Central Office had sent advisers down. He was being groomed. He visited television studios, took elocution lessons.

The following year Julian and Jane moved to an even safer seat in Buckinghamshire. Dumble is one of the smaller rural constituencies, with many quaint cottages and haystacks. People there have redcurrant-coloured cheeks and watery brains. I have only been there once, but I retain an impression of tractors, bigotry, muddy boots, Range Rovers, greed, shotguns and boundless stupidity.

I blame my deformity for the subsequent estrangement. My sister, I know, never liked me. Besides, it was easy to understand how I would be only an embarrassment at their dinner parties and garden parties and campaign breakfasts. Nowadays Julian is something of an elder statesman, silvery-haired, with twinkling eyes, a wouldn't-hurt-a-fly lovable old gentleman, whereas I am still only three feet tall and prone to wind. Julian attends banquets and constituency dinners and talks loudly and authoritatively about Africans, canals, Europe, and missiles, whereas I live alone and dine on pilchards and bread. My only interests in life are moths, earthworms and astro-archaeology. I have no hobbies. My life of insignificance at this shabby, windswept, seaside hostel is, I suppose, the very reverse of Joe's brilliant career. Only the other day I saw him on television, looking a little fatter and a little older but sounding just the same as when I knew him.

He occupies, as you may be aware, an important position in the present administration.

Its waters are blue, shallow and extensive. The Lough is marked on few maps of the region. "Look!" cried Maggie O'Neill from Brodgar. "A huge animal." And only one hundred yards away, on the otherwise empty shore. She was in a car at the time, make and model unknown. The road crossed Flint Island, off the coast of County Mayo.

When Gay's aunt read about such things she shivered. She smelled once more the rain and the heather. Patterings assaulted the hood of her bright red anorak and a dark, unidentifiable bird soared towards the distant mountains. Then her reveries were broken by the yelp of the animal out the back. She put down the bag of carrots and glanced quickly at the TV page.

The driver of the car was a Cork businessman. He was plump and merry, with a hole in his cardigan. In later years he was lean and dour, with an ulcer. How well did he know his Yeats? Not very. He braked, hopped out. SNAP! His camera was a Kodak Brownie, his film black and white.

The beast was forty feet long, to be sure. Its tail was large. It had a head resembling a greyhound's. "It was just like a dinosaur," said Maggie O'Neill. As a child she had visited zoos on more than one occasion, and could not therefore have been fooled by a donkey or a cow, let alone a tiger. Her grasp of the Mesozoic era was broad for a girl of her age. She had, moreover, accompanied her father to the dogs on innumerable occasions.

The snap was reproduced in *the Dublin Evening Herald*, 14 June 1967. Scholars who have tracked it down describe "a rather hideous monster grinning from behind a bush".

The name of the photographer has been lost. Maggie O'Neill emigrated. There the matter might have ended. But it was not to be. Gay Brunty (a name you could never use in a work of fiction, unless coarsely seeking to violate the sweet, exacting, gravitational pull of verisimilitude or to cause gratuitous offence) pedalling innocently home from Mass along that same stretch of road encountered a twelve-foot-long creature "moving in a jumpy way, like a kangaroo". Gay had an aunt in Alice Springs, who sent postcards. Her family were the first in Blab to own a television. She had watched a wildlife documentary about koalas only three days earlier. Gay always dealt her similes with precision. They emerged, invariably, from the cream of personal experience. She had no involvement whatsoever with drugs or sin. Later, a Limerick woman reported seeing a strange log bobbing and twisting in the Lough. When her husband came to look it was gone. Mick Spooner and John McNulty saw an animal run across the road. Night had fallen. The creature was covered in slime and glared at them with glittering green eyes. Other sightings occurred soon afterwards in an area of bogland four miles south of the Lough. A glowing orange object was observed in the woods near Dumbley. Investigators found strange marks in the earth and a patch of scorched grass. In September 1971 Patrick Donleavy, aged fifty-seven and of sound reputation, swore he had come face to face with an eight-foot-tall space-suited figure in his cowshed. It was glowing and had slits for eyes. Three campers from Dublin were disturbed by waves crashing on the Lough shore on a windless night. Two days later they glimpsed a hump at least twenty feet long submerge in a swirl of foam. In May 1979 the Right Honourable Margaret Hilda Thatcher, M.P., became Prime Minister of the United Kingdom, the Conservative and Unionist Party polling the votes of thirteen million, six hundred and ninety seven thousand, six hundred and ninety bipeds. The following month a delivery van struck and killed an otter on the Lough road and all further sightings of the monster ceased. The scorched grass in the woods was soon replaced by fresh green growths. The three campers returned to Dublin and became folk musicians. Patrick Donleavy died of cirrhosis of the liver. The woman from Limerick ran off to Cork with a man from Belfast who worked in Bantry. Mick Spooner was John McNulty's front-seat passenger when the latter drove into a brick wall at 76 m.p.h. Gay Brunty lost her faith and ended up in Islington with a Glaswegian boyfriend. There she became a revolutionary socialist and devoted the rest of her life to helping build a Leninist party in preparation for the day when the capitalist system would be overthrown. She sent her aunt a postcard of the stone dinosaurs at Penge, scribbling in haste on the back: "All that is solid melts into air! All that is holy is profaned! I am at last compelled to face up to the real conditions of life, and my relations with humanity." Her aunt shook her head, and was disturbed to hear a slight rattle, as of something loose and metallic in something hollow and stony. Her head ached. She was a thousand years old. The climate did not agree with her, her niece had gone mad and the news on the radio was awful, just awful. The only movie on Channel 9 that night was *On the Beach*. She'd seen it before. Much as she adored Fred Astaire ... With a long, low, elderly sigh she picked up the bag of carrots and went outside to feed the kangaroo.

The Shrinking of Theever

The violet stench of her shaven armpits, the sticky congealed glitter of her ginger hair. A shroud of overpowering royal-blue velvet. Those terrible eyes. The darkness, gathering ... The plasticity of her face on the deck of the *Antrim*, a backwards-slanting S, her lips dribbling greyish moss-soft words, snail's-trail words, and the wind-ripped hair parted into coarse strands as if a putrefying sea-hag had risen amid sulphurous bubbles from cold and cloudy depths.

A swollen smile for freckle-faced Nick, Nick Osrick, her questioner. She was wearing stout, sensible shoes with modest heels. One thing is clear. I have met her before on a number of ... There is something there that– that– *Bang!* The time she fired off a 105mm shell, her face blank, vatic. Did you notice? Those eyes, the tight corners of her ruby mouth. Brünnhilde with ear-muffs. A spasm of pleasure shivered through her iron groin as the projectile burst distantly upon Pleasant Island. Years later I saw *The Terminator* and at once – BANG! I see now that *she* was the one who strangled the goldfinch in Monkton Manor that terrible day in June 1867. And later, in 1923, the swindle in Peru amazed everyone. There was a scandal, a rumour ... Or was that someone else? I may be mistaken on one or two minor points. Although I am English, a man with good nerves and not afraid of things which live in the memory forever, I am not quite the – Memory is a fallible, gullible, malleable material. At first you remember everything, every segue and dolly shot, every word, and then the sprockets tear, the heads wear out, the actors are mute, pages go missing, an entire act, next all you're left with is commercials for your life, thirty-second good times, short, half-satisfying spurts, flashes in the head, glimmerings, and then – The years are heaped upon me like stone slabs. The darkness comes again. It is gone eleven. The clock coughs. A golden shower of dust tumbles in a patch of sunlight across a long neglected corridor.

It was, I recall, the governess upon whom suspicion's finger fell. A thin pale undernourished girl in black, her head stuffed full of nonsense about God and the aristocracy, she was despatched in disgrace, weeping, down the long drive. Her body was recovered from the lake a week later. Mordred merely smiled, brushed back her golden hair and proceeded to address Lady Broughton. Her voice was silky, authoritative. She spoke of the need for vigilance and a large militia. Her eyes glowed with a strange avidity. *Mordred Hellar Theever*. In those days she called herself Margaret Sneeker. The dogs were not fooled. Neither was the leader of the Gypsy orchestra. The dogs kept up a low growling and snarled if she came close. The musician avoided her as much as possible. It was the same in Budapest in the spring of 1938 when Professor Nemetz introduced poor Harvey Gorton to Theever.

There is a suspicious bloom to her complexion. Some of the newspapers attribute this to vitamins and strange baths. It is possible, I suppose, and yet ... Gorton's body, of course, was found to be almost entirely drained of blood.

That area of pink flesh around her lacquered brows – you have noticed it too, perhaps? A minor malfunction resulting in a fused circuit. It must have happened round about the time of the 1832 Reform Bill. By 1867 it was visibly drooping. She attempted to repair her looks as best she could using powders, a screwdriver, some 13-amp fuse wire and a dab of pink paint, but surgery was not one of her finer points, extermination, not creativity, was her forte. If, as she held the little screwdriver, her fingers shook, it was because the enhancement of life went against her deepest machine instincts.

When I say a fused circuit I am guessing. If this part of the human body was associated with the runnels and holes of the procreative process then one might well suspect impotence or even the onset of senility. There are other explanations. The physical strain exerted upon the body by an unyielding moral rectitude. An ascetic attitude to food, drink and electricity. Journalists and political scientists have evolved many explanations during the course of her long rule. Once, when drunk, B – I cannot believe any of this – confided his knowledge of a curious episode in which, wearing a blue dressing gown and a pair of floral slippers, she was said to have absent-mindedly walked up her bedroom wall at Chequers, and on across the ceiling, upside down and not a hair out of place, all the while discoursing loudly on solutions to the problems of Australia. Witnessed, B claimed, by a lewd and unreliable peeper named Thomas, one of her detectives, who, disobeying the order to patrol the grounds, climbed an oak tree by her bedroom window, hoping for a glimpse of corsetry and flesh, and who instead received his come-uppance in the unanticipated form of a severe apoplexy, brought on by what he had seen, which sent him crashing to earth in a shower of twigs and amber leaves, leaving him afterwards forever mute, confined, deservedly, to a silver wheelchair. The story only came out years later when the penitent developed an interest in tapestry.

Over the years, when discussing the Theever problem, I have heard wild talk of satanism, post-Fordism, Tunguska, Tarot packs, Hyperreality and the Glastonbury zodiac. I regard all this as gossip. The theory that Dickens knew her well, however, strikes me as being entirely possible. An oily tide of characters flood relentlessly the cellars of my imprisoned mind. It must have been during the writing of *Great Expectations* that he first encountered her. The inspiration! Consider Mrs Joe. Consider Miss Havisham. Consider Jaggers. Remember the extraordinary voices with which the silence teems ...

The darkness comes again, and with it (no thanks to Nellcock or the do-nothing officials) her voice. Her voice, her deep soft husky harsh sucking metallic imperatives booming hollowly out of boxes everywhere, across the sleeping cities, surging on across the moonlit fields and meadows. Rodents, hairs bristling, scatter in terror.

What is to be done? High explosive has been used and failed. She simply scrambled out from the smoking wreckage, spitting the dirt from her fangs, chirpy as Arnold Schwarzenegger. Her shaken wires and electronic grids reassembled themselves in moments, her claws were intact and gleaming. I do not now think it will ever be possible to entice her along a conveyor belt and crush her with industrial machinery until the green glow in her eyes is finally extinguished. *She must be shrunk.* Time is on our side. I have plotted for many a long – Leaflets through letterboxes at dead of night. Stickers and crucifixes attached to lamp-posts. Chants in the street. The distribution of garlic. Respect for picket lines. The general deployment of orgone energy accumulators. The mass mobilisation of the fuddled proletariat. Pyramid power! A general strike. Meditation in crop circles. Anything's worth a try, isn't it? But it is not enough to be persecuted. You must also, like Galileo, be right. There are signs that some of these activities are working. Lately, on television, I have observed a strange tightness on her face, as if the shrinkage had begun. Tall women are now kept at a distance. Her bodyguards have been replaced by smaller men. Last week, on the news, she appeared ill-at-ease, as if invisible threads were tugging at her lower lip, trying to drag her down to where she truly belongs ...

Have you noticed that wherever she goes, she now always wears high-heeled shoes?

(1982-September 1990)

As every young American knows, former President Nixon was born in Nausse, Arizona, at sixteen after three in the morning. What is not taught in the schools is that at a quarter after four the previous afternoon a shower of threadworms fell from an empty blue sky, coating not only Nausse and the modest log cabin where Mary Nixon sat expectant in the family rocker, but also Trud and the environs of nearby Sare.

As the deluge hit the rooftops the citizens began to hum "Hark the Herald Angels Sing", thinking it was Christmas. Then they remembered it was August and sweltering. Sweating, they ran outside, gazing in wonder at their shimmering white TV aerials. It was only when they began to stamp merrily across the white lawns beyond their porches that they began to scream. Soles slid on something softer and more slippery than ice, and as the citizens went sprawling across the six-inch-deep sea of sticky wriggling worms they realised they were far from the homely realm of fun. Hollering, shrieking, boots and coats sticky with clusters of writhing threadworm, they ran back indoors to be sick.

The stench was astonishing. Dick Nixon senior staggered back to his cabin, where his pregnant wife and his shotgun were waiting. 'What in *hell* is going on?" she cried, pressing finger and thumb together across the shapely curves of her nostrils.

"Goddam reds," sobbed Dick, scraping wildly inside his back collar, where a score of imaginary creatures tormented him.

It was Sheriff Winner who thought to telephone Washington. "The damnedest thing," he explained. "They jus' came outta the sky, covered every damn house in town. Five minutes later they was *gone* like they was never here. Except for the *smell*. I put some in mah lunch pail as evidence and dang me if they ain't ee-vayp-orated!"

"Hold the line, Sheriff," said the senior White House aide.

The aide turned to a figure in the corner of the room. "Sir," he said, in a sombre voice. "There's something pretty weird happened over in Arizona. I think this could mean the thing you told me about."

The figure in the corner of the room picked up the telephone. "Sheriff," he said. "Tell me, is there a pregnant woman in Nausse right now? By that I mean a woman about to go into labour."

"There sure is," drawled Sheriff Winner. "There's Mary Nixon, down in log cabin nine-nine-seven-eight. As decent and as purdy a woman as you could hope to meet. Sir, I hope you ain't trying to tell me she had anything to do with this *abomination*. Because if you is let me tell you–"

"Easy, Sheriff. Easy," laughed the voice on the telephone. "Mary Nixon is no more responsible for the Nausse threadworm downpour than you or I. Leastways, not in the way you mean. The fact is, we believe she may need help. Listen, Sheriff. I want you to do me – and America – a favour. I want you to go home to your sweet wife and your dear little children and sit you down in front of your radio. Open up a six-pack, listen to some of them fine cow-and-tree-and-waste-urn sangs an' forget this conversation ever happened, y'unnerstan? I want you to know you did the right thing, telephoning Washington. And just between you, me and the fence the next time the boys get round to dipping in to the ol' slush fund – well, let's just say you won't be forgotten."

"Say, that's mighty generous of you, sir."

"It's what it's all about, Sheriff. Or should I say – D.A. Winner."

"District Attorney! Hell, wait till I tell Frankie and the kids! Sir, I can't think of the words to – "

"Then don't, soldier," said the warm, familiar voice.

Five minutes later an anonymous black truck pulled out from the parking lot behind an anonymous block on the George Washington freeway. The male-midwife taskforce was on its way.

*

On a bright sunny afternoon in June in the last quarter of the eighteenth century the townsfolk of Krarp, Idaho, were astonished to see a man wearing a top hat pedalling a bicycle across the sky at a height of six hundred feet. Since aircraft had not yet been invented, let alone jet propulsion, the event caused widespread excitement and consternation.

Various attempts were made to signal to the cyclist, who took no notice and simply pedalled onwards, finally disappearing into a cloud which hung over nearby Shatner. Among those who stood in Krarp's dusty main street, gawping, was Charles Monroe, factory owner, farmer and sportsman, whose wife, Barbara, was asleep in her room. Barbara was in the thirty-ninth week of her confinement and the doctor said the baby could come any time. Monroe knew he ought to be in the house, in case she needed him, but it is not every day you see someone cycling over town at that height. Though he hated himself for what he was doing, he stayed where he was, rooted to the spot, until the rear mudguard gently melted into the cloud. Even then he could not tear himself away. Like everyone else he lingered there until nightfall, hoping the cyclist would reappear. Of course, he didn't, and Charles Monroe made his way back to his ranch conscious that he had not only wasted an entire afternoon which might have been more profitably devoted to his numerous business interests but also that he had neglected his wife.

His sense of guilt deepened when he arrived back to find the ranch in turmoil. His wife was having hysterics, the maids were running to and fro wringing their hands and to cap it all his daughter's llama had escaped.

At last they were alone together. Sobbing, her pretty cheeks glistening with interesting tear-patterns, she told him what she had refused to tell anyone else.

"Oh, Charlie, I had the most awful dream!"

She'd dreamed she was in labour. But it wasn't a baby she'd given birth to – it was an ink-horn!

An ink-horn. Her husband frowned and stroked his chin in the thoughtful way he had read about in stories in magazines.

An ink-horn. Hell, he hadn't seen an ink-horn since the time Tom Cripps had hit town with his point-thirty-eight. That was way back, when he was just a kid. He wondered if the old schoolroom in Dodge City still had the bullet hole in the blackboard. It was the day the Clancy brothers had tried to run Cripps out of town. One of the bullets had gone clean through Monroe's ink-horn, breaking it into twenty-six jagged pieces. After that he had gone over to graphite. Even now his hand trembled on the rare occasions he had to put his signature to documents.

An ink-horn. A curious name. Found, in his big purple-jacketed dictionary, between "inkbag" – the anal gland of the cuttlefish – and "inkle" – a kind of broad linen tape.

"Charles, are you listening to a word I'm saying?"

"Darling, *of course* I am."

The midwife had lifted up the ink-horn with a worried look. Her assistant stepped forward with the scissors.

"God damn it – sorry ma'am – where the hell's the cord? Say, what is that thing?"

"Oh Lawdy!"

Barbara Monroe found speech returning to her mouth. "Don't spill my baby!" she shrieked.

But she was too late. A look of indescribable revulsion crossed the midwife's face and she let go. The ink-horn fell to the floor and shattered. Thick streams of black oily ink gushed everywhere.

"And then I woke up, screaming."

"My poor darling."

"Where were you, Charles? Where were you when I needed you?"

"Darling, let me explain. I know you're going to find this hard to believe, but there was this man on a bicycle riding across the sky and – Barbara, what is it? What's happening?"

"It's my contractions. I think they're beginning! Call Midwife Kellogg! Call for crisp white towels, clean linen and a sparkling bowl of water in a creamy china basin! Get some medical onlookers! Charles, I don't mind telling you – I'm scared."

After six hours of excruciating contractions she began to dilate. "Hell, what's going on?" thought Midwife Kellogg when she saw. "That ain't right." She stepped closer to her patient. "Honey, has you bin eating lotsa beans lately?" But before Barbara Monroe could answer the midwife's puzzling question her waters broke.

"Well if that ain't the dangdest thing I ever did see," muttered Miss Kellogg, who had never married for fear of the consequences. She felt the warm glow of justification fall upon her ancient anxieties. That evening she left town forever, her head filled with dark notions about the Monroe marriage.

Things did not get any better. As Barbara Monroe began to dilate the possibility that what was happening was merely some sort of temporary setback receded. Soon the aperture was nine centimetres wide and getting wider. Inkle was brought into the room, just in case it was needed (it wasn't). Midwife Kellogg began a long, contrapuntal monologue, consisting of "Oh my God, this I do *not* believe!" and *"Push*, honey. Hard as you can!" The baby duly emerged, the cord was snipped, Miss Kellogg cried, "Honey, it's a boy!" and Barbara Monroe burst into tears. Right up to the very last moment she had been worried the midwife was going to hand her that pesky ink-horn from her dream! In the room at the end of the corridor Charles Monroe heard his son's first piping howls. He pushed the monogrammed pencil-box away from him and set aside his sharpener with a relieved smile.

The funny thing was, Miss Kellogg didn't think anybody had noticed apart from her. Except maybe the black maid who came to clean up the scraps of placenta from the floor. She was the only one who held her nose and looked carefully around the floor as if fearful she might tread on the anal gland of a cuttlefish or something equally soft and unpleasant.

"Ma'am, would it be alright if I was to take these few scraps home to fry up for mah boys? They ain't eaten for a week and youn' Jim's fair wastin' away."

"Sorry, honey. Mr Monroe made a deal with the cosmetics factory. They pays ten cents a pound for afterbirth. He expressly asked that you bag it and take it to his office. He wants to weigh it hisself."

In time the new-born infant grew up, overcame a bad stammer and became fifth President of the United States of America.

By now you will have understood the two things which mark a man out for supreme office in the greatest nation on earth. They are commemorated by a little ink-horn, made entirely of melted-down silver dollars, which stands on the large leather desk in the Oval Office. Seeing it in photographs most people assume that, like the big stick, the miniature covered-wagon and the brass replica of Tom Cripps's point-thirty-eight, it is simply a quaint memento of the old pioneering days.

You and I know better.

Backyard

*"Honey, have you seen the air-freshener? I need it real
bad."*
"Not now, babe. The President's talking."

It is raining in Mottobbe, Ohio. Suddenly a shower of live frogs
hits every street from West 25th to East 19th. "The damnedest
thing you ever did see. Mary-Lou and me was listening to that
there radio when next thing – " The all-male-midwife-task-
force is there within the hour. "Let me see that map." "Wadd-
aya say her name was?" "We're here!"

"Who the – "

"Take it easy, Mr Reagan. We're here to help. Take a look at
our authorisation."

"Gee, sorry fellers. You know how it is nowadays. Only the
other day there was these strangers in town. They didn't look
like Americans, they didn't dress like Americans, they didn't
talk like Americans 'n they sure didn't *smell* like Americans.
Folks reckon they was South Americans, mebbe from Peru or
Barcelona or some place. All we know is next thing the Grants's
rabbit was gone *and* the Polks's kangaroo. What's more, when
the Hoovers came back from a barbecue at the Wilsons they
found their llama missing."

"Their *llama*?"

"It's a South American ally of the camel. Here boys – take
this wad of ten dollar bills. Why don't you all go buy yourselves
some beers and a nice, fat dictionary. You'll find 'llama'
between 'Lixivium' – water impregnated with alkaline salts –
and 'llanero' – an inhabitant of a llano."

"A *what*?"

"A vast level plain in South America. You know how it is with
folk from those parts. They read too much Proudhon. I guess
they thought they had a moral right to the llama. But that don't
excuse what they did with the rabbit and the kangaroo. Hell, if
they was hungry they could have fried up some frogs."

Tremulous female voice: "Who is that at the door, Chuck?"

"It's the team of male-midwives from Washington. Come along in, boys."

"Thanks, Chuck. And now that we're here, I want you to go back to your walnut-veneer radio and listen to some big band music. Well look after the little lady from now on. Don't be alarmed if you hear screams. You just relax, take it easy. We'll have the little feller out in no time."

"Sure thing."

"And here's a little something for you and Mary-Lou."

"Gee, thanks. Say, what is it?"

"A silver ink-horn. Courtesy of the United States government. For your mantelpiece."

"A silver ink-horn, huh? Mary-Lou and me never had one of those. You see, Ma and Pa never had too much dough. Mom worked in a dime store six to six, Pa scraped penge from the pipeline bolts until his nose was blue and our little dawg Virgil, our dear blessed little dawg – "

"Later, Chuck We have work to do."

The deputy assistant midwife injects pentothal into Mary-Lou. The task-force leader puts on his scuba-diver's outfit, reaches inside Mary-Lou and slides his rubber-gloved right hand under the infant's puny buttocks. He tugs and hauls. Secret Agent Harrison slips in the forceps and heaves. The future President squeezes out like a half-suffocated pot-holer, florid and contorted. He opens his lips and dribbles, howls. He is gifted with clairvoyance and candid blue eyes. He gurgles. Through the shutters he can see three men. Men from across the border. While the household is distracted by the birth of the new-born child the intruders cut through the walls of the stables with a specially sharpened peanut-butter knife and make off with the horses.

"Glaaaarg! Yeeeoooh! Ugga-warg!"

But no one understands.

"He's a cute little feller," says Harrison, smiling.

"You got a name for him, ma'am?" asks the task-force leader.

"We surely have," grins Mary-Lou, "We aim to call him

Raan."

"That's one hell of a name!" chuckles the third member of the team, justifying his now redundant presence by some cheap, throwaway dialogue.

"Oh my God!"

"What is it, ma'am?"

"Look! The stable door! Someone's taken my horses!"

"Well, ma'am," says the task-force leader. "I guess there's no point in bolting it now."

While Harrison goes to call the cops the baby closes its eyes and falls asleep. The black maid comes in with a brush and dustpan.

"Excuse me, ma'am," she says shyly – but Mary-Lou interrupts. "I know just what you you're going to say, and the answer's no. That placenta will fetch eight cents a pound down at the farmer's market. Chuck and me need every last cent we can lay our hands on so's we can pay for a new electrified wire fence. I know your boy Jim's wastin' away, and I'm sorry. You should tell that lazy good-for-nothin' husband of yours to crawl out of bed and do some work for a change. My poor daddy didn't stay at home in bed – he went out and scraped penge off pipeline bolts until his nose was blue. When he died in agony from an industrial disease at the age of twenty-nine he made sure there was some of that real nice life-insurance for his poor widder to collect."

"But Dick can't go out and scrape penge. He's black. And besides, he ain't got no legs!"

"He should learn to sew. There's money in sewing."

"But Dick ain't got no arms!"

"He's got a mouth, hasn't he? He could become an entertainer. He could whistle toons. There's gotta be summpun he could do. You tell Dick to pull himself together and stop whingin'. Whingin' never won no wars. Now please clean up that afterbirth and quit botherin' me, Betsy!"

"Yes, ma'am."

*

32

During the first twelve months of his life the future President spends much of his time on his stomach, fouling his diapers and thinking about the missing horses. Their names were Champion, Rosebud and Hemingway.

His early life. Cowboy hat, holster and shining ... Shirts put him on the road to success. He whistles toons at the Greyhound station and accumulates dimes from impoverished yell appreciative travellers. Everyone seems to like the handsome boy who can perform a trumpet solo of "Rhapsody in Blue" through his nose and tap out "Somebody Loves Me" on his teeth. Later he goes into movies and plays the part of Sheriff Good in *Revenge of the Clancy Gang*. Politics beckons. When asked why he says something about a rabbit, a kangaroo, a llama and some horses. After his inauguration he is presented with *El Gran Garrotte*. It has been passed on from President to President ever since the time of Monroe.

The stick is for using in the backyard. The backyard's trouble – big trouble. The President senses the chaos down there, tangible as snowflakes. There's reds down there in all kindsa shapes. He can smell 'em. They flash before his eyes, jittery and sparkling. And dust ... cacti ... dangerous snake-infested ruins ... Lizards. The yard's a jungle. It's full of places he can't spell, let alone remember. Places impossible for a man to pronounce. Hell, they don't even speak American down there. He hums a few bars of "In a Mist". He's starting to feel excited now, angry even. His emotions are getting the better of him. As a child he once saw some red ants crawling up the kitchen waste pipe and emerging near his Mom's fridge. Inside the fridge was his birthday cake. The cake had a marzipan fort on top and toy soldiers dressed in the blue of the Seventh Cavalry. The ants were headed for the rubber lip under the fridge door. He got there just in time with the kettle from England and the boiling water ... He remembers all the movies he was in, all the movies he's seen. He's seen the horror pics, he knows what to expect. They can't fool him. He knows that at nightfall limbless hands scuttle among stilled American machinery. Nuke 'em, boys! Splatter 'em to hell!

The stick on his desk is heavy and powerful. He lifts it up, swishes it through the air. Abruptly he slams it down on a potted cactus from Salvador, crushing it. He pushes the remains on to the floor and stomps on them. He's determined to teach that splattered cactus a lesson it won't forget. Soon there's a green ooze all over the carpet. Not to worry: it's time for the black maid to come in and clear up the mess.

The technicians arrive with their wires and arc lamps and microphones. The make-up girl powders his cheeks and puts rouge on his lips.

"Like this?"

"Yes, sir, Mr President. That's fine, sir."

The President gazes at the nation with decayed graveyard eyes. He is old and tired, his voice a velvet whisper. His blue eyes are streaked and bloodshot. Someone smelling of mint-flavoured toothpaste is smoothing pink paste into the cracks around his eyes.

"Try not to move your face muscles when speaking, sir. We don't want no accidents."

"Uh-huh ..."

"Sir!"

"Yes, boy?"

It is one of his aides.

"Try to remember your days doin' commercials, Mr President. All the time you's talking you try thinkin': *I am holding out to these good folk the joyous promise of a backyard clean as a crisp new shirt*. Think you can do that, sir? Remember – American imperialism and the military-industrial complex are countin' on you."

"Heck, I sure try," the President says. "But *thinkin'* the same time as you's *talkin'* ... that's a pretty tall order, son."

"You just do your best, Mr President. If anything goes wrong we'll cut to the puppet. Hell, we did that once before and nobody noticed."

The President absent-mindedly fondles the silver ink-horn on his desk He thinks of his long-dead mother. The loss of those horses broke his poor Mom's heart ... His mind slips gear. He wonders if his dietician will let him have cheese-burgers again today. He wonders what's coming up on TV that evening. Then he remembers: he is.

But right away he forgets all about that crisp white shirt. He's seven years old and worried about that cake. He's in a panic, he's hollerin' for his ma ... He's boiling the kettle. He has to exterminate those ants!

"On the air in thirty-seconds, sir."

He focuses on the opening words on the cue. MY FELLOW AMERICANS ... He thinks: a good beginning. Solid. Trad-itional. Full of reassurance. Reassurance and solidity is what folks like.

The red light goes out and the green one comes on. The actor in him takes over. He looks up, like the camera crew have breezed into his study and caught him spontaneously bowed over his desk. Behind him, on the fake shelves, row after row of painted spines display a pleasing symmetry. To some viewers they are encyclopaedias, to others dictionaries.

The President opens his mouth and the sounds come squeezing out.

Dobson's Zone

Matters of war are more subject than most to continual change.

Miguel de Cervantes Saavedra,
The Adventures of Don Quixote

One measures a circle, beginning anywhere.

Charles Fort, *Lo!*

1

Dressed in combat gear, merging with the landscape, high up on the hillside, crouching, tense, expectant, waiting ...

Who now remembers Che Guevara?

There was a time when it seemed as if every college student in the Western hemisphere had the same large scarlet poster taped to the wall above the bed. Che's young, handsome face, framed by black curls, the famous black beret with the red star badge ... The Doors and the Stones and the Incredible String Band poured from the speakers, a stick of incense trailed a thin blue sweet sickly trickle of smoke across the room, there were late nights and extraordinary mornings, endless coffees, and endless talk of Marx and Mao and Marcuse, revolution, poetry, giant newts, plesiosaurs, the death of the novel, and music, music, music. And all the while comrade Che was with us, paying no attention to the distracting activities taking place on the bed or on the floor, looking out across the room through a pale screen of fumes, seeing some distance beyond the window the plump mauve-complexioned Dean of Students (who was soon to be extinguished at a stroke, aged fifty-three, by an out-of-the-blue hammer-blow coronary), crossing the empty walkway in the rain, his *Daily Telegraph* tucked under his arm, muttering to himself, a worried, anxious look upon his face ...

Giant newts? Plesiosaurs? Yes, plesiosaurs. And giant newts. In the 1960s everything seemed possible. Even the likelihood of a living herd of plesiosaurs (or possibly a lonely giant newt) paddling to and fro in a rather narrow lake beside a main road in one of the most densely populated nations in the world ...

On June 12th 1967, high up in the hills of Bolivia, Che and his group of guerrillas, knowing nothing of plesiosaurs or giant newts, set out on a long march to the Grande river. It was a grey, overcast day, and by late afternoon the weather had worsened. A strong south wind brought a night of cold and rain. The next day, June 13th, the going was hard and the group marched on for only an hour, to the next watering place. They had just enough food for five days.

At Loch Ness the morning of June 13th 1967 dawned bright and clear, and the loch was as flat and calm as a mirror. The group leader at the headquarters of the Loch Ness Phenomenon Investigation Bureau looked out of his caravan window and saw that conditions were perfect. Whether or not plesiosaurs prefer warm weather and are drawn to the surface with the salmon, or whether they are simply easier to see in those conditions, was a conundrum unendingly and enthusiastically debated at the local bar at the end of a long, tiring monster watch. The group leader was committed to the second theory, although, as all investigators ought to, he retained a half-open mind and was perfectly willing to be persuaded of the other man's point of view, provided that the facts were there.

The team was roused, and the watchers, binoculars always at the ready, set off in their green Bedford vans to their surveillance posts at selected lay-byes along the north shore of the loch. There the powerful 35mm motion-film cameras would be taken out and set up on tripods on top of the vans, and the watcher or watchers would unfold aluminium garden chairs, sit down, tune their transistor radios to the Light Programme, and, dressed in combat gear, merging with the landscape, tense, expectant, waiting, begin the long day's gaze ...

At that time of the year volunteers were scarce (numbers would rise substantially in July and August) and each observation point had only a single watcher. It was a risky procedure, for if a plesiosaur erupted out of the dark waters while the observer was off the platform brewing tea valuable seconds would be lost in hurrying back to the camera, getting the lens in focus and on target and pressing the correct button. It would be no use the observer swearing that the object had been unmistakeably a huge, living creature, at least forty-eight feet long, with two dark brown humps, the suggestion of powerful flippers and a bearing and demeanour unquestionably identical to that of the supposedly extinct marine dinosaur portrayed in the Natural History Museum postcard which was pinned to the wall in the crew's mess – not if all that the witness could back up his astonishing assertions with was some rather grey, scratchy film of what looked like nothing more than a windrow or at best a boat's wake. No. What was required was stark, unambiguous motion film of a gigantic unknown animal, proving beyond all doubt that the so-called "Loch Ness monster" was not hatched from human folly or the requirements of a tourist area suffering from economic recession and the closing-down of the local railway and steamer routes but something very wet and very real. "The right man in the right place at the right time" – that was the slogan that ran through each observer's mind when the sheep woke the crew, baa-ing stupidly or urinating loudly against the caravan walls in the doubt-nurturing emptiness of the night.

At 11.40am G.M.T., at the very same moment that troops of the Bolivian army were searching for Che Guevara, the observer stationed at the camera point opposite the tiny village of Dores saw an unidentified object cutting across the surface of Loch Ness, leaving behind it a vivid wake. He began filming. Almost at once a second object appeared in the viewfinder, on a parallel course. It was the tourist boat, *Scot II*. Instantly the first object appeared to accelerate and crash-dive.

When Dobson first arrived at Loch Ness the following week he found the atmosphere at Bureau H.Q. still electric with excitement. Word was the beast was in the can! That would make the sceptics choke on their laughter!

Having made a careful study of the subject prior to travelling north, Dobson was an upholder of Gould's by then unpopular giant newt theory. Even at the age of nineteen Dobson was a fanatical book collector, and he had snapped up the original June 1934 edition of Lieutenant Commander Gould's now classic *The Loch Ness Monster and Others* for two shillings and ten pence in a long gone second hand bookshop in South Street, Chichester. Like most other people in those days Dobson had heard of the famous monster, without ever thinking very much about it. Gould's book proved to be a shattering experience, for it demonstrated almost beyond any shadow of doubt that Loch Ness contained at least one gigantic unknown animal. Witnesses had seen as many as eight humps on the creature, and it seemed to be anything from forty to sixty feet long.

The sentence which, more than anything, sent a shiver along Dobson's spine, was this one: "A vastly enlarged, long-necked, marine form of the newt is the hypothesis which, however improbable it may appear, I should personally be inclined to favour, and I am glad to note that it has recently been endorsed by Mr Malcolm Burr, D.Sc., in *The Nineteenth Century*." Even the sceptic is likely to be stopped in his or her tracks by a statement like that. Smiles, smirks and other facial antagonisms may well find themselves ebbing involuntarily, helpless before the powerful recognition that the statement was not only not made lightly but emanated from a Lieutenant Commander in H.M. Royal Navy (Retd.), a man who had knocked about in some pretty odd corners in his time, a man who was nobody's fool, and who was, moreover, backed up by a Doctor of Science. And while Dobson had never come across *The Nineteenth Century*, it sounded like a reputable, balanced publication, in an altogether different league to, say, *Punch* or that new magazine called *Private Eye,* which you couldn't get in any of the newsagents but only from the man with the eye patch and the rather grubby raincoat who stood all day in the shadows of the railway bridge by Portsmouth Central, his interesting little collection of foreign magazines and fringe publications spread out on the pavement before him.

2

Even in those days Dobson was a striking figure. Aged nineteen, he looked nothing like Che Guevara, except perhaps for his unusual height, which he perversely exaggerated by wearing elasticated boots with massive Cuban heels. His hair was silvery-grey, he favoured yellow corduroy waistcoats and out-of-fashion collars held in place by a gold pin, and he stuttered. Dobson also had the unusual habit, injurious to his frail grasp on good health, of carrying an enormous rucksack of books around with him wherever he went – even if it was just a few yards down the road to post a letter. Dobson did not like to talk about this, but it seems that ever since reading about the mysterious and devastating explosion, equal to a thirty megaton bomb, which occurred as a result of an unknown projectile from space hitting the Yenisei forest in a remote region of Siberia at 7.16am local time on 30 June 1908, he had lived in mortal terror of being caught out by a similar event and of having nothing to read. At the age of twelve Dobson apparently constructed a home-made computer considerably in advance of its time solely for the purpose of working out the statistical probability of his being within a one hundred metre range of a good bookshop or library in the event of the abrupt extinction by powerful explosion of that intricate accumulation of wires, tubes, drains, sound stages, prisons, armaments factories, dockyards, museums, germ warfare establishments, arterial highways, exhaust pipe repair workshops, galleries of American expressionist art and sundry other artefacts popularly called Western Civilisation. The odds were not good. Hence the khaki rucksack.

Although I was not able to see more than a fraction of the books in his sack that bright morning in late June 1967, I did manage to spot his yellow-jacketed Gould, a copy of the Corgi paperback edition of *Lolita* bearing an encomium from the DAILY EXPRESS ("writing of tremendous vitality and variety of mood and texture. Everything is here, cruelty, learning, robust humour, pathos, romanticism, true affection"), a couple

of books – *Maquis* and *Horned Pigeon* – about the 1939-45 war, the *Selected Poems* of T. S. Eliot, the first Penguin paperback edition of *Under the Volcano,* a Heinemann Educational edition of *Gulliver's Travels* carrying the heartwarming information, "A number of passages which might be considered offensive have been omitted from this edition", the first December 1965 edition of the Signet Classic text of William Shakespeare's *The Comedy of Errors,* with extracts from Shakespearean criticism, including Hazlitt's observation that "This comedy is taken very much from the *Menaechmi* of Plautus, and is not an improvement on it. Shakespear (*sic*) appears to have bestowed no great pains on it ...", what, if I was not very much mistaken, was the Norwegian translation of *Jude the Obscure,* the Pelican edition of I. A. Richmond's *Roman Britain,* an abridged edition of Frazer's *The Golden Bough,* a volume of the love poems of Ovid, translated into English, a large, battered one-volume Oxford English Dictionary, a Webster's, a Nuttall's Standard Dictionary of the English Language, a brand new hardback Roget's Thesaurus, the 7/6 Fontana paperback of *Doctor Zhivago,* with a full colour photograph of Julie Christie on the back cover, a novel which, according to *Time* magazine, showed that not even Communism could destroy a people's hopes and humanity, and lastly the four-shillings-and-sixpenny Penguin anthology *The New Poetry,* with Jackson Pollock's "Convergence" spread across the front cover, spine and back, reproduced by permission of the Albright-Knox Art Gallery, Buffalo, New York. The froth on the surface of Dobson's vast pool made my own holiday reading – a *Selected Poems of Thomas Hardy* and a copy of *Titus Groan* – seem faintly risible.

For six mornings Dobson rose at dawn and I drove him to one of the camera points along the loch. After his first day at the loch he abandoned the idea of a solitary giant newt and was converted to plesiosaurs. He watched with extreme concentration and enthusiasm, in a state of tense expectation, his bulging sack of books at his feet and his forefinger never far from the ON button of the Newman Sinclair. Birds which

neither Dobson nor I knew the names of crossed the sky, or crouched on twigs, defecating and making implausible noises.

We became friends, united perhaps not only by our love of books, our indifference to foliage, strange grasses, butterflies and animals, but also by our silences. I have never much enjoyed talking, believing it to be, like television, a dangerously slick, fallacious method of communication (apart from the not insubstantial medical dangers inherent in excessive lip fatigue and abuse of the jaw muscles). Talking is for politicians and those who deal in second hand cars, life insurance and double glazing. Lovers get by with passionate glances, caresses and the transmission via maids and loyal valets of billets-doux, babies find screaming a perfectly adequate method of ordering a meal or a drink, drunks manage to survive with the aid of a mumble, a vomit and the occasional hearty belch, and those of us not ashamed to call ourselves intellectuals live out our lives amid the pleasures of solitude, assisted only by the printed page and, at most, pencil, typewriter or ballpoint pen, and the occasional exchange of a card or teasing cryptogram.

If Dobson had lived longer I feel sure he would have become as keenly interested as yours truly in British Sign Language. As it was he got by with nods and winks and, when absolutely unavoidable, the occasional stuttered word. I well remember how one morning a line in Hardy's poem "The Convergence of the Twain: Lines on the loss of the *Titanic*" struck me as peculiarly apposite to our interest in sub-surface matters, and I quickly scribbled down on a piece of paper, "The sea-worm crawls – grotesque, slimed, dumb, indifferent", and then handed it to Dobson. He glanced briefly at it then indicated that he wished to borrow my pencil. I passed it over and watched with muddily beating heart as Dobson annotated my message. He wrote fast, very fast. I gazed, dazzled, as at the centre of a silent universe the sharp point of graphite looped and zig-zagged across the white papery void in a blur of speed which in retrospect strikes me as very reminiscent of a twenty-four pin dot-matrix printer set in the draft mode. Then he passed the scrap of paper back to me.

Greedily I devoured the riches he had laid before me: "Sinking of the T trivial compared to Tunguska. But give me sea-worms any day to people. Strange how both disasters begin with a T. Convergence an interesting word. Bears various meanings apart from collision course, including confluence, assembly, focalization, coming to a point, tangential and vanishing point. The opposite of divergence – contradiction, going apart, divarication, parting of the ways, crossroads, ramification."

On our last evening together, drinking whisky, and then more whisky, and then yet more, I have never forgotten how we came (whose idea was it – his or mine? I no longer remember) to open up his Thesaurus at random, selecting quite arbitrarily a single, humble word, and chuckling as our fingers promiscuously roamed back and forth across the pages, up and down, between and below, touching every inch and scrap, every glorious, throbbing vowel and consonant and crackling, pulsating fiery connotation, until at last, drenched in sweat, half-drunk, utterly fatigued by our endeavours, we tumbled into a wordless, innocent and dreamless sleep. Ah, what it is to bathe in language, to cavort there, unashamed, ecstatic, up to the very ceiling of one's mind in beauty and resonance, drifting and gliding amid the harmonic choruses, the plangent chords, hearing the sweet hum of pluralism, soaring across the dazzling ranges of multiplicity, then falling, falling, dizzy, satiated, drained and drowsy, soothed by excess of meaning! (Chess, by contrast, has always struck me as rather a bore.)

Our last evening ... and then divergence, divarication, the parting of the ways. Next day, instead of rising at dawn to watch the loch, we departed with our headaches and our luggage to Inverness railway station. In my mind I can still see Dobson, sweating with effort as he hauled his bulging sack along platform 3, and groaning mysteriously as he boarded the Lowestoft train. He had failed to catch a glimpse of the monster, yet his faith (despite that groan) seemed undimmed and in its prime.

3

Some days later I received an envelope postmarked Great Yarmouth. It contained a short letter from Dobson, dated July 6th. This, of course, was the very day that Che and his men left Barchelon and headed for Pena Colorada. While I sat in the shade of a weeping willow, sipping lime and lager and watching the sun slip away behind my parents' privet hedge, Che was getting closer to the Alto de Palermo. I went indoors and watched television. At ten I went upstairs, brushed my teeth, and went to bed. I re-read Dobson's letter and then put out the light. I fell asleep. Little did I realise then that, while I slept barely above sea level in my parent's quiet Bognor villa, Che and his men were descending from 1,600 metres, heading for the nearest grocery store.

Is Pollock's "Convergence" structured or is it merely a random splattering of paint? Is there balance there, and pattern, secret symmetries of colour, lurking surprises, strange discoveries, teasing testimonies to brilliant brush-strokes? Or is it just a mess, a mockery, a confidence trick of the trade?

I expect somewhere there is a book that gives the answer. I wish now that I had looked Dobson in the eyes and bluntly put these questions to him. At the time, knowing his distaste for the spoken word, I kept my silence, and now I am doomed until I die to wander a bleak Dobson-less terrain, a wilderness of infinite bewilderments and moss-coated regrets.

It was Dobson who told me what occurred after Che's visit to the grocery store. The plan was to seize a vehicle coming from Sumaipata, drive to the chemist's shop there, raid the hospital, purchase some tins and sweets, and then return.

In the event no vehicles came from Sumaipata. Instead six of Che's men stopped a lorry that was coming from Santa Cruz. No sooner had the lorry been halted than the plan began to go wrong. Another lorry drove up. They waited, tense, silent, for the lorry to go by. The lorry slowed down and the driver stopped to offer help. Che's men seized the driver. But the driver was not alone. A fierce argument broke out between the revolutionaries and a woman who had been travelling on the lorry with her daughter. The woman, quite understand-ably, had no wish to see her daughter leave the relative safety of the lorry's cabin for the unknown dangers of a Bolivian road at night, especially when the notion had emanated from a group of ruffians with names like Coco and el Chino. How was she to know that these men were revolutionaries, motivated by a well intentioned desire to transform Bolivia from a corrupt puppet state governed by yankee imperialism into a socialist society free from squalor and exploitation?

At this point a third lorry came along the road. The driver quite naturally stopped to see what was going on. By now the road was completely blocked. Almost at once a fourth lorry arrived on the scene.

Is Pollock's "Convergence" about the chaotic unravelling of plans and structures? Does it offer a droll comment on the nature of loose endings in the post-modernist era? Am I fooling myself when, in the top left hand corner of the painting, I see a partial representation of the course of the rivers Piojera and Angostura, balancing, in the lower right hand corner, what looks very much like the route of the railway line just north of Boyuibe? Dobson would have known – and now it is too late, too late, too late.

4

In his letter (which, surprisingly, made no mention of Loch Ness or the monster) Dobson explained that he had been offered a place studying English at the University of East Anglia. He gave me the address of his flat on the Unthank Road in Norwich and said he hoped I would keep in touch. I wrote back at once giving him the news about my place at Portsmouth Polytechnic, where I was to embark on a Cultural Studies course.

To my surprise I saw very little of Dobson over the next ten years. I had expected him to make the journey up to Loch Ness the following summer, but my letter suggesting we monster-hunt together went unanswered. While my enthusiasm was just as great the next year, and for several years afterwards, Dobson, astonishingly, seemed to have lost all interest in the subject. I was at first bitterly disappointed that I would not be seeing him again, and later I was hurt that he did not answer my letters. It was not until the first anniversary of Che's death, long after the cameras had been unscrewed from their sturdy wooden tripods and put away for the winter, that I received a reply which explained his remarkable indifference to the Loch Ness monster. Dobson had become a revolutionary socialist!

Life, he explained in a letter which I will never forgive myself for mislaying, was too short to waste in pursuit of empty chimaeras. (Dobson was still evidently fond of words and dictionaries.) Apart from the fact that anyone who hoped to take life seriously was required to read – where available in translation – the collected works of Marx, Engels, Luxemburg, Lenin, Trotsky and Mao (which in 1968 stood at four hundred and seventy-eight volumes, with many volumes still outstanding), there were innumerable urgent matters to attend to, including attendance at picket lines, demonstrations and union meetings, as well as paper sales, the pasting-up of posters at night, weekly meetings, study sessions and the annual summer camp. If there was any time left over it had to be spent on brushing up his Norwegian and learning French, German, Spanish and Italian. If, between the hours of 2am and 5am he had time to spare, then he allowed himself to relax with a good book – *Joseph and his Brothers,* say, or *À la recherche du temps perdu.* The letter concluded with an invitation to meet him in Trafalgar Square the following Saturday at noon.

Was it Dobson's idea of a joke that he omitted to inform me that a quarter of a million other people would be there? Probably not, probably he was simply tired and had completely overlooked the fact that I had no idea which of the fringe Trotskyist groups he would be associating with in that turbulent sea of red flags and shimmering banners. Gazing down from the low wall in front of the National Gallery I found the scene momentarily reminiscent of that tortuous canvas by Pollock. Blobs of black, swirls of scarlet, a curling trail of yellow ... For a while I wandered among the crowd, looking for a tall figure dragging a sack of books. I was dimly aware of booming, indecipherable speeches washing across the square, mutilated by gusts of wind. A ... MERRY ... CAN ... PEARLY ... CHASM! ... VENOM! ... WHIRR! ... HOOT! HOOT! HOOT! pockets of the vast crowd seemed to be shouting. I pressed on through the throng. No sign of Dobson. Then, suddenly, the crowd thickened, pressed more tightly together, and I realised I was trapped. Next moment we were off, surging like a great river through central London. I remember a flag being burned, fists raised in the air, chanting, a line of policemen lunging at us with raised truncheons and contempt and hatred in their eyes ... While others bravely fought back, I pulled out my copy of *The Great Orm of Loch Ness,* held it over my head, crawled between the legs of a constable and scuttled like an escaped lobster up the nearest side street.

5

Dobson wrote three days later to say that he regretted he had not been able to attend the demonstration as he had had to go into hospital for an operation. He envied me my good luck in having been there and promised to get in touch when he was fully recovered. I wondered if his illness – unidentified – had anything to do with the weight of his sack.

As it turned out, I did not see Dobson until December. He telephoned, inviting me up to Norwich for the weekend. That was the first shock: Dobson had become a keen talker. His stutter had vanished, and as we walked from the railway station to the bus stop I was astonished by the fluency of his discourse. The second shock was the absence of Dobson's book-crammed rucksack. He no longer limped or gasped as he moved, but trod the cracked asphalt surface briskly, bombarding me with statistics, quotations, angry information and argument.

Unemployment had reached half a million and was rising – the highest for twenty-seven years! The Labour government had abolished free school meals for the fourth and subsequent children of large families, simply to save a miserable £4 million! In London thousands of tenants of the G.L.C. had marched against a 7/6d rent rise to County Hall. In Londonderry the police had brutally attacked civil rights marchers! Meanwhile the wars of imperialism – Vietnam! Biafra! – went on and on.

In truth, Dobson was in danger of becoming a bit of a bore. I could read all about that sort of thing in *The Guardian*. It had nothing to do with me. I had no desire to reproduce myself once, let alone four times. Large families invariably signified Catholic parents, in the grip of absurd superstitions. If they chose to spurn pill, coil or sheath, that was their affair. Admittedly the 7/6d rent rise sounded a bit stiff, but somehow I did not think that if the rise was abandoned the tenants would rush off and spend the money on a Pasternak novel. It would doubtless be frittered away on beer and cigarettes and broken-down second hand cars. In any case, I reflected, exasperated, there were other, more important things in life – for example, the identity of the Loch Ness monster.

"There's a new theory," I said. "A chap called Ted Holiday reckons Nessie – he calls the beast an orm, by the way – is nothing less than a unique evolved form of giant marine worm. He's written a book proving it. Apparently over in the States they've recently discovered a new fossil, *Tullimonstrum gregarium*. Admittedly the largest known fossil is only fourteen inches long, but Holiday reckons it looks just like Nessie. You've got to admit it's a pretty fascinating idea."

"The sea-worm crawls – grotesque, slimed, dumb, indifferent, eh?" said Dobson sardonically, athletically springing aboard a cream-coloured double-decker which waited for us, silent and empty, by some railings.

At first I had no idea what he meant, and then I remembered.

"As a matter of fact, old sport, we know quite a bit about the sinking of the *Titanic*. Your Thomas Hardy puts the whole thing down to a mysterious convergence of ice and ship organised by a couple of pseudo-mystical entities called 'The Immanent Will' and 'the Spinner of the Years'. The fact is, there was nothing mysterious about its sinking. It sank because of commercial greed in the pursuit of the Blue Riband. The ship was travelling too fast and too far north. It sank with heavy losses because third class lifeboats were left out to boost profits. The figures speak for themselves. Sixty-three per cent of first class passengers were saved, while seventy-five per cent of those travelling third class were drowned. The *Titanic* was a floating symbol of capitalism. They might have just as well called it *The Herald of Free Enterprise* or something like that. And when Hardy drivels on about 'No mortal eye' being able to foresee what was going to happen, he's talking as much garbage as your man Holiday. The Loch Ness monster can't possibly be a giant evolved marine worm because there's no such bloody thing! What's more, no one's ever filmed the back of a gigantic unknown animal at Loch Ness, all they've ever filmed is an out-of-focus boat a long way in the distance while in a state of extreme stress. Read their books, for God's sake! Half these people are going through a mid-life crisis! They don't want to go on being aeronautical engineers and living in a bloody semi-detached in Reading. They want adventure! They want to hunt dragons! Who can blame them? Capitalist society exploits us, alienates us, twists and deforms us! It creates false needs! And if the need to look for extinct marine dinosaurs in a bloody lake in Scotland isn't a false need then I don't bloody know what is!"

6

We passed a cinema showing *Wuthering Heights* and a Green Shield Stamp shop. I gazed hotly out at a bird crouched on a wire and a man walking by in a blue raincoat. It was starting to rain.

To get to Dobson's flat it was necessary to walk along a side street off the Unthank Road, and plunge down an alley deep in long grass and a trail of domestic refuse. Up the alley was a gate, through the gate was a scruffy backyard containing two metal dustbins and a jungle of weeds. A track of crushed thistles led to some wooden steps, at the top of which was a black door, the panels of which someone had once begun painting green. Dobson shared the flat with two or three others, none of whom appeared that long wet weekend. Whether they were elsewhere, or simply in a horizontal stupor in their rooms, I never knew. Dobson gave the front door a vigorous kick, and it creaked open.

Inside lay dust, darkness and the most astonishing collection of empty bottles I have ever seen. The furniture seemed to consist largely of wardrobes, upon the tops of which were stacked brown suitcases, hat boxes and numerous old biscuit tins. The vague memory of a film in which Albert Finney plays the part of a homicidal maniac who keeps a severed head in a hat box on top of a wardrobe surged briefly in my mind, then rapidly ebbed.

Dobson's room contained an enormous pine double bed with a salmon-pink cover, a boarded-up fireplace, a Bush gramophone with one of the new "stereo" speaker attachments, and a rickety chest of drawers. Half a dozen chocolate-brown cushions were scattered around a faded rug and about thirty LPs were stacked against the far wall. Above the bed a poster of Che Guevara was attached to the wallpaper by golden drawing pins. It was the first time I had ever seen what was to become one of the biggest selling posters of the next five years. On a small bedside table lay an open Green Shield Stamp book, half filled. By the bedside lamp a cutting from a magazine had been sellotaped to the wall, and I went over to see what it said. As I closed the door behind me the doorknob came away in my hand. Dobson seemed unsurprised by this. Taking it from my hand he pressed it back into the hole in the door. Then he went off to make coffee. The cutting said:

WANTED

ONE HAROLD WILSON
FOR THE FOLLOWING CRIMES:

Gun running to Lagos; terrorizing and black-mailing
British workers and students; colluding with racists
Smith, Vorster, Callaghan, Nixon.

Height: none. Nationality: Sicilian.
Distinguishing features: smug expression and a
sanctimonious whine.

Dobson returned with two thick china mugs and handed me the purple one with ARSENIC printed on the side. Without a word he went over to the record player and for several hours we listened to Simon and Garfunkel, the Doors, Leonard Cohen, the Rolling Stones, Deep Purple, Fairport Convention, the Incredible String Band, Donovan, Bob Dylan, Van Morrison, Tom Paxton and The Velvet Underground.

When the music stopped Dobson pointed at the record player and said in a low voice, "It was the Which? Best Buy, you know." He added with a smile: "If you are capable of trembling with indignation every time that an injustice is committed in the world then we are comrades."

I was not at all sure that I was, but he told me Che's story anyway. When he had finished he went over to the chest of drawers, pulled out a pamphlet and gave it to me. "You can keep it," he said The pamphlet repeated much of what he had just told me. It ended in a flurry of exclamations.

Guerrilla warfare in Bolivia is not dead! It has only just begun! Che's dream will be attained through armed struggle, which is the only dignified, honest, glorious, and irreversible method which will motivate the people! No other form of struggle is purer. Guerrilla warfare is the most effective and correct method of armed struggle! Guerrilla warfare in

Bolivia is not dead, it has only just begun! Bolivia will again resound to the cry of VICTORY OR DEATH!

"Thanks."

7

I did not see Dobson again for ten years. In 1973 I made my last visit to Loch Ness. By now the Investigation Bureau had closed down and I camped in some woods on the south shore. Dressed in combat gear, merging with the landscape, high up on the hillside, crouching, tense, expectant, waiting ... My vigil was in vain. It seemed the monster or monsters had outwitted everyone, including me. In 1974 I met and married Matilda. Matilda adored dancing and abhorred Scotland. I loved to waltz with her. She had an Australian accent (although born in Berlin she had been brought up in Darwin). Matilda and I embarked on an epic, whirlwind tour of half-empty dancehalls in seedy seaside resorts. I learned to thrill to the music of the Palm Court Orchestra and the sight of salt-blighted tropical plants languishing in pots. Matilda wore polka-dot dresses with yellow spots (ideal for someone like her, who lived off soft-boiled eggs and who, although she did not know it then, had Parkinson's Disease). She was thrillingly, throbbingly alive. We were young and in love. We laughed at each other's jokes, we kissed and caressed and caroused, we danced the night away and drank champagne at dawn. We loved as no one has ever loved. The following year, amid rage, tears and much broken chinaware, unable to stand each other's presence for a moment longer, we divorced. If I mention Matilda at all it is simply to show that during most of the nineteen-seventies I became preoccupied by other matters, to the almost total exclusion of plesiosaurs possessed of Scottish nationality.

I say almost. My old interest in the subject flared up again when, in the autumn of 1975, it became known that an astonishing sequence of extraordinary underwater colour photographs had been taken at Loch Ness by a team of American scientists earlier that year. When they were published they created a sensation. One showed an animal with a rough, red-brown skin and two appendages – obviously flippers – estimated at thirty to forty feet long. A second showed the underbelly of the monster with what were evidently parasites hanging from it and a dark patch which was described with gentlemanly delicacy as "possibly the creatures anal fold". A third, the most sensational of all, bluntly identified by one expert as "the most remarkable animal photograph ever taken", showed the monster's head, in stark close-up, from a range of only eight feet. Its mouth was open and inside was what appeared to be teeth; two horns protruded from the head, and the face was divided by a bony ridge. It was hideous, unnerving, amazing, stunning – and every feature of the face precisely matched the contours of the fossilized remains of a plesiosaur!

If I had not met and fallen in love with Martha Saxby I would probably have rushed off back to Loch Ness and spent another fruitless fortnight scanning its dark and enigmatic surface. But Martha made it clear she had no truck with plesiosaurs. She was a member of the Militant Tendency and if I wished to go on sharing her affections there would be no time for nonsense like that. She enrolled me in her local Labour Party branch and let me in on the great plan. Having de-selected the local MP (a rather slippery character named Eric Eel) and replaced him with a Militant, the Parliamentary Labour Party would in time be transformed, would nationalise the top one hundred companies, and would bring the capitalist system to heel, inspiring the devotion and enthusiasm of the broad mass of toilers whose minds were at present temporarily drugged by tabloid newspapers, sport and television.

What happened in the course of the next six years would make a novel in itself, although I do not think I shall ever write it. I quickly tired of the Labour Party and all its tendencies and instead devoted my spare time to the lives of the Brontës. Martha fell out with her comrades over their attitude to feminist tapestry, abandoned the revolution, became bored with weaving, and started a subscription to *Flying Saucer*

Review, thereafter spending long hours of the night in our back garden with an astronomical telescope and a gleam in her eyes. There, crouched between two dustbins, she displayed the same gritty commitment and devotion to the cause as once went into standing outside the local post office clutching a thick pile of unsold copies *of Militant.* In November 1978 she left me, and ran off with Dennis, a ley-line enthusiast from Dorking.

Glumly, I went away to review the wreckage of my life. Taking nothing with me but six packets of Kendal Mint Cake, a life of Emily Brontë and three Leonard Cohen albums, I rented a house in Glastonbury for a fortnight. Each morning I climbed the famous Tor and gazed out at the misty distances, my life a Martha-less blank, my mind a film theatre showing continuous performances of The Life and Times of Martha.

On my last morning as I panted up the steep slope to the summit I saw that there was a solitary figure already there. It was, of course, Dobson. We recognised each other at once, although I am not sure how we managed it.

"What! Are you here?" he muttered in a rather distracted way. He looked terrible. His eyes were sunken, his hair white and thinning. There was a long, white scar under his chin, as if he had successfully fought off an assault by a maddened Fundamentalist wielding a scimitar. He was wearing sensible corduroy trousers and a navy blue duffel coat.

"Still looking for plesiosaurs?" he said, with a sardonic smile. I flushed and grunted something about the slow accumulation of the evidence.

"Still trying to overthrow capitalism?" I added, rather feebly.

Dobson ignored this. "Looking back," he said in a low voice, "I am struck by the curious similarities between the activities of the Loch Ness Phenomenon Investigation Bureau and Che Guevara's little army. The attempt to prove the existence of a large unknown animal, the attempt to overthrow the regime in Bolivia by guerrilla warfare ... Both missions involved young, long-haired men dressed in combat gear, with a romantic, sixties, everything-is-possible attitude ... and both missions were, of course, doomed to failure. Take a look at what Che wrote in his "Analysis of the Month" for June 1967 – that very month, my dear friend, that you and I first met! *The almost total lack of contacts continues ... The morale of the guerrilla stays firm and the will to fight increases.* There are curious parallels, are there not? Failure heaped upon failure, and the refusal to see that the whole enterprise was doomed from the very beginning. The quickening of morale and commitment in such a context has an oddly religious ring to it ... and then the notion that all one needs is the right publicity ... *if it can be proclaimed widely, it will be a great factor in enlightening people.* Rupert Gould or Che Guevara? And these illusions are in the end dangerous, for they breed cynicism, despair, apathy ... What has happened to the glorious mood of the 1960s now, eh, my friend? It has fizzled away into a lot of nonsense. Lyotard and Baudrillard, post-Fordism, the world made safe for Nietzsche and NATO. In effect the assimilation of the young radicals into capitalism accompanied by despair, helplessness ..."

"So what are *you* doing nowadays?" I enquired, to change the subject.

"As a matter of fact, I am searching for immortality," he replied.

"Ah," I said, uncertain of how to respond. I wondered if Dobson had joined one of those sects run by Rolls-Royce-owning charlatans with long hair and massive beards.

"By means of a zone. Or, if you like, a joke."

8

I did not understand, and said so. Dobson put a finger to his lips and said: "Later." Then, in silence, he led me down the Tor to the field where his gypsy caravan was parked. His horse Engels was tethered nearby, cropping the grass and occasionally swishing his tail. We went inside and Dobson poured two glasses of whisky, which he proceeded to drink. Then he poured two more, and a third for me. He explained briefly that since we had last met he had been married twice, had seven children who lived with their mothers in Crete and Doncaster, and had purchased the caravan from a film company which was closing down. It was, in fact, the caravan used in the making of Powell and Pressburger's wonderful *A Canterbury Tale*, and although he would rather have had the Mini from *The Satanic Rites of Dracula*, it was all he could afford.

"Now about the joke." A glow came into Dobson's eyes as he began to explain that if a man wanted his name to endure after his death, and if he had neither the talent to paint, nor to compose a symphony, nor to write a major world novel, nor to overthrow a state in the name of the people, nor the strength to erect in interesting patterns standing stones weighing forty tons each, then he ought to manufacture a mystery. But for a hoax to be successful and to endure after the perpetrator's death various essential ingredients were required.

"It must be entirely novel, yet with hints of an ancestry. It must be baffling yet plausible. Once visible it must be constructed so as to encourage the mystery-mongers and occult-property-speculators to heap up a vast tower of rickety theories. It must entice the imagination and encourage a throng of competing, mutually exclusive explanations. It must be stupidly simple to invent yet give birth to generations of commentary. It must be a labyrinth which entices the seeker-after-truth to enter, and then imprisons her in a wilderness of perplexing and half-possible speculations. It must, in short, provide a Z.C.F.M. – a ZONE for the CONVERGENCE of FECUND MULTIPLICITY. The productions of such a zone will range from the crudest scepticism to a sixteen-volumed explanation replete with photographs, sketches and innumerable eyewitness statements. It must ..." But here Dobson gave a strange groan, and fell silent. A prominent blue vein which ran from his left temple into his bleached hair began suddenly to mimic the flutterings of a cabbage white which had appeared at the window. "My joke," he eventually managed to whisper, "began last year."

Towards midnight Dobson told me what he had done. In the second week of January 1977, after Cordelia had taken the children, the Cortina and the credit cards, and left for Doncaster, he had eight nights in a row experienced a recurring dream. He was standing on a hillside looking down at a circus when, suddenly, a tremendous storm broke overhead. Thunder thundered, lightning crawled across the sky, torrential rain crashed down and a fierce wind began to tug impatiently at the straining ropes of the big top. Spectators and performers burst out of the exits and ran off into the night, as the circus tent broke loose, whirled away into the sky and vanished. At once the storm ended, the night ebbed and the noonday sun burned down on the empty arena. Gazing down at the circle of yellow sawdust, Dobson felt a sudden powerful sense of well-being. He turned, and there beside him sat Che Guevara, handsome, smiling, alive, with a semi-automatic machine pistol tucked inside his trousers. He held out a Polaroid photograph. "This is it, amigo," said Che. "No one could argue with *this*." He passed it across. There in the picture was the Loch Ness monster, in full profile, with a yeti seated on its hump. The yeti (female, full-breasted and with a demure smile) was holding on to reins attached to the monster's neck. In the background could be seen Urquhart Castle. Above the castle's ruined tower hovered a silver flying saucer about the size of a double-decker bus. From one of the windows of the saucer stared the face of Harold Wilson. He looked worried about something. Judging by the position of the dark shadows on the blue water beneath the castle walls, the photograph had been taken at about two-fifteen in the afternoon on a Tuesday in July.

"A stupid and meaningless dream," Dobson added, "but it gave me an idea. Have you ever heard of the mystery of the devil's footprints?"

Apparently one winter's morning in the nineteenth century people living along the Cornish coast woke up to find large, mysterious prints in the snow. They began by the estuary at Fowey and went in the direction of Lostwithiel. Not only were the prints unlike those of any known animal or bird but they ran in a straight line, over hedges, walls and rooftops, for fifty-seven miles, before abruptly terminating in the middle of a forty-acre field. There seemed to be no natural explanation. That it was a hoax seemed impossible. It was a genuine and never repeated mystery. Known as the mystery of the devil's footprints, it had lingered on over the years in books devoted to such arcane matters.

"Now, amigo," said Dobson, parodying his dream-Che, "take a look at this."

He handed me four black and white photographs. They each showed fields under snow in rural landscapes devoid of people or buildings. In each field could be seen a dark circle where the snow had either melted or been crushed. The remaining area of each field was unblemished and footprint-free.

"You will have noticed that each photograph bears a number on the back. The first was taken near the village of Dumble on February 8th. The second shows Tanner's Bottom six days later. Number three shows a field below Warminster Hill, March 14th. The last one was taken from half-way up Glastonbury Tor on April 1st. Oh, and there's also this."

He handed me a cutting from the *Shaftesbury Advertiser*, April 10th 1978.

CIRCLE BAFFLES FARMER. Farmer Derek Archer says he is baffled by a twenty-foot-wide circle of melted snow which appeared in a field of barley on his farm last week. "I've been farming here for forty years," he told our reporter, "and I've never seen anything like it." Police said they had received no reports of helicopters in the area, and as no damage had been done they would not be taking the matter any further.

"The joke," said Dobson quietly, "has begun. Would you like another whisky?"

"But how – Do you mean to say that *you* – ?"

Dobson raised his forefinger, tapped the side of his nose and winked. "Not now," he said. "Some other time." He took the photographs and the press cutting and slipped them into a foolscap envelope.

The next day Dobson still refused to discuss the matter and I

58

returned to Leytonstone not a little irritated by his teasing silence. As happens in all the best narratives, my work (which involves chiming hammers and sixteen-millimetre projection – I will not baffle you with the complex details) took me back to Glastonbury a few months later, and I decided to look up my old friend. This was easily accomplished, for he was once again seated by the Tor's summit, and as I approached from below that cold late May morning I had a clear view of the greyish fluff interlaced with strands of scarlet cotton which clung to the inside of his turn-ups. Dobson looked old and ill. When I asked what the matter was he said simply, "No snow."

We descended to the Syringe and Quoit, where we swiftly drank ourselves into a stupor. "It's all gone wrong," Dobson muttered. The mild winter had ruined everything. He had completely overlooked the rapid depletion of the ozone layer with the ensuing global warming – a process which seemed likely only to be accelerated by the newly elected Conserv-ative government, deeply committed as it was to the internal combustion engine and major reductions in the factory inspectorate.

We parted with a brief handshake by the statue of King Arthur. "You must understand that my commitment to the overthrow of capitalism is unwavering," Dobson said. "The future seems to me to be full of possibilities greater than any we have glimpsed throughout the past ..."

Two nights later he phoned me up. It was half-past-two in the morning. Dobson sounded drunk. "I've cracked it!" he shrieked. "I've got it all worked out. It's perfect. A minor modification! Instead of midwinter it's midsummer madness! Why I never thought of it before I'll never know!"

"I have no idea what you are talking about," I muttered angrily. "Don't you know what time it is?"

"I'm talking about my joke! My immortality! My zone!"

"Not now, Dobson."

"I won't tell you what it is. I'll send you something. I want you to promise not to open it for nine years."

"For God's sake –".

"Promise!"

"Okay, I promise. Anything to get back to – ".

The line went dead.

9

A week later a large brown recorded delivery envelope arrived from Dobson. Inside was a slightly smaller large brown envelope marked NOT TO BE OPENED UNTIL JUNE 1987. I slipped it into an empty file at the back of the bottom drawer of my filing cabinet and promptly forgot all about it.

I heard nothing more from Dobson and my work took me north, not west. In 1980 I met Norah and we set up house together. I did not return to Glastonbury until four years later. It had been a fabulous summer and the sky was azure, my cheeks lobster pink and the hosepipe ban still in force as I drove west through a parched landscape of fields recently devastated by yellow combine harvesters. I drove into Glastonbury, left my car at the Camelot car park, and made my way to the Syringe and Quoit. I think I half expected to find Dobson inside, bowed over a crumpled paperback, three empty glasses on the table, the half-congealed froth in each glass slipping and slithering in fits and starts down the plastic sides, constructing strange white galaxies inhabited by complex life forms (my mind – my scrupulous, dazzling mind – instantly conjured a sketch for a nine-hundred page sci-fi saga about a vast, dying empire in the far corners of the universe which learned that the riddle of its destiny lay on planet earth, and which despatched a hero through time to unravel everything, a hero who, once upon the earth, promptly forgot all about his mission and instead became an abstract impressionist painter, calling himself "Pollock", and whose muddy and miraculous canvases endeavoured to capture the blurred, spectacular, colourful view from the time-capsule moments before acceleration tumbled him into oblivion, whereupon the empire sent a second hero, who discovered the horrifying truth, that the empire was simply the fading froth in Dobson's third glass, and who, even as he saw the shocking truth, was too late to prevent the barmaid scooping away the relevant glass and obliterating ten million complex endeavours with a wanton burst of tap water). But Dobson was not there. Dobson was not there for the simple reason that the Syringe and Quoit was not there. It had been demolished to make way for the Avalon Centre, an indoor neon-lit emporium through which the visitor might wander, along an aisle lined with potted plastic spider plants, lost for choice amid Guinevere's Grill, Lancelot's Leathergoods, Merlin's Menswear and King Arthur's Kitchen. I turned on my heel, found it an intoxicating experience, turned three or four more times, was cautioned by a security man, and fled to the Tor. I was in luck. The Tor had not yet been levelled in order to construct a bypass or a car park, and I hurried up the steep, familiar slope. In the field below I could see white blobs which formed plausible representations of rabbits, evidently frightened by something. In the next field two white horses galloped towards a distant gate. It was a still, silent morning, and no birds sang. I continued along the narrow path, Humming "Jerusalem" to keep my spirits up. I did not seriously believe I would find Dobson there at the summit, fluff still clinging to the inside of his trousers, so you can imagine my surprise when I saw his familiar, Dobsonish profile stencilled against the blue sky. I say *you can imagine my surprise* and retract it at once. How can you possibly hope to imagine even a shred of my rich, complex, inner life? Besides, my unimaginable surprise gave birth to a yet more un-transmittable wealth of emotion when Dobson turned, and I saw that it was not him at all but a bearded man with a pair of X7 binoculars around his neck and a chart of the zodiac held in his right hand. Beyond him, just over the brow of the hill, stood a party of Japanese, a couple from Texas, and a second bearded man. I asked number one beard if I might borrow his binoculars for a moment, and scanned the countryside below.

The sedge had withered in the pond by the A361. The sky over Dumble had the rose colour of Stalin's acne. Smoke was rising from numerous fields, as farmers carried out the old country tradition of incinerating the stubble. Soon the air was thick with the oily stench of blazing gasoline and scorched earth. I kept the field of vision moving in a slow circle, like the long, opening shot of Roeg's *Far From the Madding Crowd*, and soon spotted Dobson's unmistakeable figure. He was walking along a country lane, keeping close to the hedge, holding an orange Sainsbury's carrier bag in his hand.

The car was a dark saloon. Whether or not the driver was an abstract expressionist or a carpenter will never be known. In the last months of his turbulent life Jackson Pollock drove like a maniac, but anyone with experience of our roads knows that the building trade produces just as many crazed, stupidly dangerous drivers as romantic art. The car was a squat, dark bullet on a collision course with Dobson. As I explained to the police, I can tell at a glance the difference between an elasmosaur, a plesiosaur and a giant newt, but to me Fords and Peugeots and BMWs are all just cars. It was a car, a black car, and it was going far too fast. The concept of pedestrian use of the highway was clearly alien to the driver (as it is to so many drivers). Dobson couldn't see what was coming. The convergence of fast car approaching the bend on the wrong side of the road and innocent pedestrian, the inevitability of the collision, was visible to no one but myself, 292 feet above sea level, looking down on everything like God.

It happened very quickly. Dobson might have been an Evenki nomad, strolling through the Yenisei forest at 7.17am on 30 June 1908. He was tossed up over the bonnet, bounced along the roof of the car, and then fell, at speed, head first, on to the shimmering asphalt. I tried to focus on the car's number plate but the lens was a misty blur and my hands shook uncontrollably. A thick, acrid cloud of smoke swept unexpectedly across the scene, blotting it out. There was a sudden, astonishing, unexpected lightning flash, a dramatic clap of thunder, and then the rain began bucketing down. I thrust the binoculars back at their owner and began running down the Tor.

10

On 7 July 1967 a man who lived in a sugarcane field sold Che and his band a pig. The man seemed friendly. Che wrote, "I wanted to extract some of his teeth, but he preferred not to have it done." Where is that man today? Where are his old, rotten teeth? Where is the man with the eye patch who sold fringe publications under the railway bridge in Portsmouth? What happened to the man in the blue raincoat, hurrying through the Norwich rain? On 7 October 1967 an old woman goat herder blundered into the hiding place of Che and his depleted comrades, and was taken prisoner. Three of the guerrillas went to the woman's home, where she had one crippled and one dwarf daughter. She was given 50 pesos and told to tell no one that she had seen them. Then the seventeen comrades set off by moonlight along the canyon, leaving many tracks. On the radio they heard that the army had the guerrillas encircled by 250 troops between the Acero and Oro rivers. *The news seems to be a red herring*, wrote Che. Those were the final words in his diary. The next day Che and his men were discovered hiding in a narrow ravine, and surrounded by a large body of soldiers. Che was wounded and captured. He was taken to the nearby village of Higueras. After twenty-four hours of captivity he was machine-gunned from the waist down. He did not die. Later he was shot with a pistol.

Dobson was luckier. He died instantaneously of multiple injuries. I did not attend the funeral. I had no wish to meet obscure aunts and uncles who lived on different planets, and who had never hunted plesiosaurs or plotted the overthrow of capitalism.

I returned to Kidderminster, and Norah. There I found a note waiting for me in the bedroom of the empty house. "Remember Dicky, who mended the lawnmower and who was interested in royal ghosts? We are in love. I am leaving you. Do not try to find us. Farewell – Norah."

I gazed at the note in stupefaction. What on earth made Norah think I could possibly want to pursue her? I was over the moon. I let loose a loud whoop – then, out of respect for Dobson, I chased the whoop around the room, silenced it and put it back in its cage.

And so the years go by. Norah never came back to me and I never heard from her again. Eric Eel, of course, is now the Opposition's Front Bench spokesman on the environment (and the part-time director of a company specialising in the disposal of nuclear waste).

I live alone, childless yet happy. My hearing has virtually gone, my vision has grown dim. Though almost totally immobilised, I have taken out life membership of the Pedestrians Association. It is, I think, what Dobson would have wanted.

And now it is time to look back, to sum up, to put a frame around the chaos. What is there left to say?

Once, I remember, Dobson described an amusing episode involving a visit made to the University of East Anglia by the distinguished thinker, writer and politician Roy (now Lord) Jenkins. This was during the time of the Nigerian civil war, when Jenkins was a senior member of the Wilson government. As Jenkins began to speak a device resembling a gigantic clock was wheeled on to the stage behind him. Perplexed, aware that one or two people in the audience were beginning to titter, Jenkins mopped his brow and glanced back to see what was going on. All he could see was a board with numbers on. But as he spoke the numbers began to change. A young man in the audience stood up, shook his fist at Jenkins and screamed, "MURDERER!"

"As I was saying – ".

But more and more of the audience were getting up, more and more students were shaking their fists and shouting. "Murderer!" "War criminal!" "Child murderer!"

The board was a score board. As Jenkins spoke the score board calculated how many Biafrans had died during each minute of his speech, as a direct consequence of government policies which Jenkins supported. As the dead rose in a metaphorical heap behind the politician's portly figure,

Jenkins's face (which even then was a hideous mix of mottled mauve and blackcurrant blotches) became even more discoloured. The meeting broke up in disorder.

The scoreboard was Dobson's idea. I think it was probably the most brilliant moment of his life – surpassing even his zone.

Dobson's zone?

There is no such thing, of course. It is impossible to prove. Feel free to dismiss it. It is merely one more "explanation" amid a score or more. Perhaps the phenomenon is, as Cory ingeniously asserts, the consequence of excessive watering of crops using an old-fashioned circular irrigation machine, or perhaps Meaden is right (although I do not think so), and it can simply be put down to an as-yet-unknown-to-science axisymmetric body of ionized gas known as plasma with usually (but not always) a vertical axis of rotation.

All I ask is that you consider the facts.

By 1980 the Loch Ness Monster had finally expired. The film of a wake shot in 1967 turned out to be the only success in a ten-year surveillance – and that probably showed only an otter. The full colour underwater photographs turned out not to be of plesiosaurs but the rotting remains of trees lying on the bed of the loch. The monster's hideous head was dragged to the surface and found to be an old tree stump. There was not a scrap of evidence left which would have convinced anyone other than someone with severe learning difficulties, or an American science professor. The Loch Ness Monster is dead! Long live crop circles!

Crop circles?

Strange circles of flattened wheat!

They began to appear in the Wiltshire area in 1980. They re-appeared in 1981 and 1982. At first there were only a handful, later they multiplied like rabbits. More than one thousand cases have now been recorded, and hundreds photographed. They range from the size of tractor tyres to that of roundabouts on the A1. They have spread across twenty-six counties. They have crossed the border into Wales (but, strangely, not Scotland). They have begun to be seen in the United States,

France, Italy ... They no longer appear exclusively in wheat but in barley, oats, rye, sugar beet, maize, and tobacco. Now they are no longer simply circles or double circles or big, planetary circles attended by small moons. Now they have developed rectangular arms, astonishingly reminiscent of Spanish windmills ...

It was only the other day that I remembered the foolscap envelope. The contents were, I regret to say, something of a disappointment. I have no idea what Dobson thought he was playing at by sending me a child's inflatable ring, a tiny bag of sand, half a dozen stalks of straw and photocopies of Kafka's "The Giant Mole" and Borges' "The Circular Ruins". It was, I suppose, his idea of surrealist humour. It must have been a similar impulse which caused him to leave me in his will a small blue plastic model of a plesiosaur and (bafflingly) a pair of stilts.

It is late and I am tired. Little remains to say. Sometimes I take down from the shelf my world atlas and look at the map of Bolivia. It is a cat, ears pricked, alert, watching something. It is the face of a man with ragged hair who has been taken into custody, and the purple-brown mountain ranges of the south west are the ugly bruises on his cheek and chin ... It is the obscure, throbbing heart of a continent gasping for breath, with an American boot pressed to its throat.

I cannot recall reading anything about Bolivia in the newspapers for a long, long time.

Che and his extraordinary example are constantly growing in strength throughout the world. His ideas, his portrait and his name are banners in the struggle against injustice by the oppressed and exploited and they arouse passionate enthusiasm in students and intellectuals everywhere.

Not any more, Fidel. Nowadays, wading through rivers and crawling through undergrowth with an M2 is not regarded as the way to go about things. No one advocates rural guerrillaism as the most attractive route to socialism in the modern epoch. Nowadays, if you drop by at someone's house for coffee and a chat about the best anti-imperialist strategy, chances are national liberation through guerrilla struggle won't even be mentioned. The reason is, of course, that it long ago became evident to anyone with a scrap of intelligence that the development of a powerful working-class movement based in the factories and the formation of independent working-class organisation culminating in the seizure of power by the proletariat supported by the mass of toilers and organised into Soviets is vastly preferable to guerrillaism or Castro's Cuba, with its complete lack of any of the fundamental organs of proletarian power.

It is late, and I am old, old and tired. You will by now have noticed the scar beneath my chin ... Since my throat operation I can scarcely speak. I am bruised, I bear the marks of old, painful injuries. I live, like my dear Uncle Toby, amid the memory of old campaigns ... I will never return to Loch Ness, never again wheeze my way up Glastonbury Tor. If I was a much younger man I expect I would hurry to the nearest crop circle and walk around inside it, taking photographs and jotting down important measurements. I would thrash out with my comrades the correct strategy for solving the mystery. We would stride briskly to the summit of a Wiltshire hill with our X7 binoculars, and crouch there, in combat gear, merging with the landscape, tense, expectant, waiting ...

Memory, sweet memory.

I will always remember that last evening at Loch Ness, when Dobson and I opened up the Thesaurus. The word – the marvellous word! – we hit upon, quite by accident, was DELUSION. Delusion is unfactual, unhistorical, wide of the truth, devoid of it, unsound, implausible, fantastical, ill-informed, coinage of the brain, crinkum-crankum, falsehood, flight of fancy, jiggery-pokery, wangle, swiz, red herring, hoax, bluff, spoof, leg-pull, diversion, hocus-pocus, insidious, collusive, bogus, sophisticated, not natural, work of fiction, extravaganza, vagary, whimsy, rhapsody, imaginative exercise ...

I have never forgotten, never really understood, Dobson's sigh and the strange wink he gave me as he finally closed the book.

The Mould

"I do wish this mould would stop spreading across Europe!" Delmore was chewing his fingernails.

"And I wish you'd stop doing that!"

"It's that mould. I can't help thinking about it. I think about it all the time."

"Listen, Del. It said in the newspaper that the mould wasn't anything to worry about. It said the dangers have been greatly exaggerated."

"But Amsterdam! Zurich! This mould sounds like it's totally out of control!"

"FOR THE LAST TIME WILL YOU STOP CHEWING YOUR NAILS!"

"Sorry, pet. It's just that ... what I mean is *I wouldn't mind if you could scrape it off*. But you can't. You've seen those pictures on the news."

"Listen, Delmore. The Government has said it's nothing to worry about. A little soap and water ... And besides, what's so wrong with purple skin? You should take a look at your back in the mirror one day. Brown freckles – ugh!"

"I don't know ... There was that science Professor. He said soap and water wasn't any good."

"He was a troublemaker. He's been arrested for Breaching the Tranquillity. The Labour leader has said he fully supports the Government in what they did. They had no alternative. The man was just upsetting people. He was asking for trouble."

"OK. So if it's all a lot of fuss about nothing you tell me why the entire royal family have gone to live in California!"

"Delmore, you have such a suspicious, negative mind. I worry about your attitudes, I do really. Sometimes I feel you'd benefit from analysis. Honey, why don't you let me telephone Dr Grey? Delmore, why are you laughing? What's so funny?"

"I already phoned the surgery. I wanted to see Dr Grey about getting some sleeping tablets. Want to know what they told me? Dr Grey flew to Chicago yesterday. So I asked for an appointment with Dr Black. They told me Dr Black is in New Zealand on vacation. So I said, OK, I'll see Dr White. Unfortunately Dr White has just got a new job in Antarctica. The surgery is closing down for a while. You know what that means, Deborah? It means the rats are leaving the sinking ship! It means the rich and the powerful are leaving us to the mould!"

"For God's sake, Delmore, will you please shut up about the mould. There's other things in life than the mould!"

"Not to me there aren't. And you haven't answered my question about the royal family. I mean – *California!*"

"Delmore, they are not well people. The Queen has anaemia. The Duke is suffering from excessive grey pigment. The Princess Royal is in a state of erratic fatigue, poor dear. Prince Charles has been getting severe twinges from an old polo injury. Diana – bless her! – needs to put some colour into her cheeks. The Yorks wanted to give their children a holiday in the sun. What could be more natural than that they should all want to get away together and put their feet up? God knows they deserve it. And as it said on the news, it means they can have their palaces re-decorated in their absence. What's so funny about that? We went to stay with mother in Tonbridge when Mr Stone and his boy came to install the shower. It was you who said you didn't want to be in the house with builders around. You said it would spoil your concentration."

"But that was for a weekend. Not a goddam YEAR. Christ, Deborah, you are so naive. A year from now you, me and forty or fifty million other people are going to be covered in purple mould! And it doesn't just turn your skin purple. There's the furry growth over everything, including your fingernails and your teeth. OK, so what's a skin-colour change? I'm no racist – I could live with purple skin. But furry growth – never. Don't you see that a year from now is when they'll tell us very sorry they were wrong and we've all only got six months to live and the royal family have decided to stay on in Malibu for another few months. Don't you see? They *know*."

"Delmore, I don't think I can take much more of this. It's like your whole personality has warped. You aren't the Delmore I married."

"I'm sorry, pet. It's the mould. It's getting to me. It's beginning to drive me out of my mind. It's like it's already here. Sometimes in the night I can I almost feel it spreading over my body."

"That's ridiculous. You watched the news. The mould has only spread as far as Belgium. It isn't expected to reach Lowestoft until the Thursday after next."

"That's what they *say*. But I don't trust them. I think they're lying. I think the mould is already here. It's a bit too much of a coincidence that all roads to East Anglia are closed for road works. I tried ringing Dora in Norwich. All I got was a recorded message saying there was a fault on the line. Yesterday I tried driving to Heathrow. There was a police roadblock on the motorway. You had to have a pass to get through. When I asked what sort of pass they became abusive. They weren't the usual police. They had semi-automatic weapons and were wearing chemical warfare outfits. I drove back to Ealing and tried to get to the airport on the Piccadilly line. There was an announcement that all trains were terminating at Hounslow Central. And you know something? None of this is on the news! The rich and influential are flying out by the plane-load all day long and the rest of us aren't being told!"

"Fingernails, Delmore."

"Sorry. It's just – it's the ENORMITY of it that gets me. And nobody seems to care! Look at what happened to the Swiss alps. I mean, Jesus. That sort of thing worries me."

"I never liked Switzerland. All those stupid languages. And so expensive. I for one shan't miss it."

"Deborah, how can you *say* these things? We had our honeymoon in Lausanne, or have you forgotten?"

"It was a dump. It was dead. And we were overcharged for coffee – not once but twice. Just thinking about Lausanne makes me feel like a good stiff drink. Honey, be an angel and go fix me an Alaska. And remember, the yellow Chartreuse and three ice-cubes, not four like you did last time."

"Deborah, it is only eight-thirty in the morning. Your drinking is getting totally out of control."

"That's because YOU are driving ME to DESPAIR. If I hear one more word about that MOULD I swear I'll SCREAM. I'm sick of it, do you hear me? Sick of it!"

"It's a good job Lenin didn't have a wife like you."

"What's that supposed to mean?"

"What I mean is you just don't understand the seriousness of the situation. People are turning mouldy all over Europe and you just plan to stay here drinking yourself silly and waiting to turn purple."

"I don't know what's come over you, Delmore, truly I don't. You never used to talk to me like this."

"The mould! That's what's come over me, you stupid, stupid woman!"

"I'm BORED by your mould. I need that drink."

"It's not MY mould. It's Europe's. The world's! And the big question is: WHAT IS TO BE DONE?"

"Have a drink, that's what!"

"Somehow I don't think science is going to come up with an answer. Organised resistance by the working class doesn't look like it's going to be much use, and yet ... Begin building a democratic-centralist revolutionary party on Leninist lines with the aim of organising effective resistance? That would certainly give me something to do. At least I'd feel good, doing that."

"Right, I'm going. I'm on my way."

"Where, Deborah? Where are you going?"

"The drinks cabinet. Then if you don't quit talking all the time about the mould I'm going back to mother. I can't take much more of this."

"Don't go, Deborah. I think we should stick together. We have to keep watching out for purplish tinges in each other's faces."

"Can I fix you anything? You want a beer or something? It might be the last thing I ever do for you, Delmore."

"Not now, pet, I'm thinking. There must be others who feel like I do. If we could get together and assist the proletariat at the right time it might prove possible to overthrow the structures of the capitalist state and set up instead a workers' state based upon councils of workers' delegates and workers' militia. Perhaps at the very last moment the mould will be held back by salt water. Boundless possibilities open up before us. Let us adopt a slogan, something along the lines of PESSIMISM OF THE INTELLECT, OPTIMISM OF THE WILL. Let us cast aside despair and look to a glorious future! Yes, Deborah, I will after all have that beer! Put "The Red Flag" on the record player and let's jive! Would you mind if I whistled? Deborah, are you listening? Can you hear me out there? Deborah, answer me. Why are you taking so long in the kitchen? DEBORAH! Deborah, if this is a game I'm not laughing."

Hitler and the Aerostat

Da-da, thumpa-thumpa-thumpa, dah bam! She is listening to her favourite Abba track. Her slender fingers tap restlessly on the sofa's walnut arm. In some ways she is looking forward to the tour. Autobahns sound fun. She loathes immobility, frogs, icicles, silence and igneous rock formations, and the Foreign Office have assured her that she will be burdened by none of these things on her trip.

Willi Schmid was in the news. The music critic for the *München Neueste Nachrichten*. A man who found politics a bore. He had a wife, three pretty children and a cello. What more can a modest man desire? Music calms the soul. The first movement of Schumann's Concerto in A minor, for example. Naturally Schmid had heard something of the government's new policies. Hardly his concern. He was practising spiccato bowing when the S.S. kicked down the door to his apartment. Such manners! And the scratches on the paintwork, not to mention the cost of new hinges! The cello, an emotional instrument, crashed to the ground with a howl and fractured its end-pin. They dragged Schmid off, still clutching his bow, to Dachau, where they broke the bow then tortured and shot the man. "How horrid!" the Princess thinks.

All a mistake! The wrong man! It was Wilhelm Schmidt they were after, not Willi Schmid at all! A minor clerical error, a mistake anyone could have made. All those spikes in the German language, not to mention all those Schmids and Schmidts in the München telephone directory. And weren't his parents just a teeny-weeny bit to blame? *Wilhelm* – so very *common*. One cannot seriously expect the authorities to be perfect. The musician's body was returned by express coffin to the distraught widow and the sobbing children. An expensive one, too, with gleaming gold handles featuring inter-linked ivy leaves and (a thoughtful touch) embossed with brass quavers. Hitler – "I really am most upset about all this" – sent his sincerest condolences. Rudolf Hess dropped by. "Good news, Frau Schmid! Your worries are over. The Führer has granted you a state pension."

The *Times, Telegraph* and *Mail* back the royal tour. Nellcock quells the militant mutterings to his rear and backs it too. Bill Blunt, the electrician's leader, calls the Princess "a girl with grit". Exports will benefit, jobs be created. Hitler has other advantages. He is constructing a bulwark. This can only be, like mothballs, a good thing. Hurrah for the royal tour!

The Princess frowns. What on earth is a bulwark? She tells Plomer to bring her a large dictionary. Plomer waddles in and waddles out and waddles in again. His thumb worms its way among the words. "Bulwark" lurks between "Bulse" (a bag of diamonds) and "Bum" (to make a humming noise, as a bee). A bulwark is a ship's side, above the deck. Strange. She did not know Hitler was of a nautical bent.

Before Plomer goes back to his wardrobe on the fifth floor (where he lives with his cat Andrew, his toy tug, his pug, his rug, his mug, his fug, his jugs, his drugs, his bugs and his slugs) he proceeds to tell her the meaning of "Bumbleputty" (a game with racquets and a tennis ball slung to a tall post, the players of which seek to hit the ball so as to wind it spirally round the post and prevent each other doing so) and "Bummel" (an aimless stroll), until driven out by squirts of hairspray.

The Princess shudders and frowns. "Führer" is an even worse word. Difficult on the tongue and impossible to spell. *Führer*. The horrid stuffed shirts at the Foreign Office have insisted she practise until she gets it right. *Few-rrruh!* On the morning of her departure she has her legs waxed by Kenneth (or "Ken of South Ken" as he is known to his clients). Ken, a roguish sparkle in his eyes, dyes her lashes a bold stormtrooper brown. Her private de Havilland lands at teatime. As she steps from the plane the band of the Labour Service strikes up the British national anthem. *Da-da-da-da-da-da-da-da-da-da-da-da-da-da-dumb*. Suddenly she is shaking *him* by the hand.

First impressions. Confused. So many soldiers and flags. He has flair, style, a velour hat. His riding-whip, flexible yet assertive. His leather shorts and open trench coat: manly, yet somehow mysterious. Mouth expressionless beneath the little brush of a moustache. Face thin and pale, and above the base of his nose, between the curve of thick brows, a clotted bulge. Ken would have something to say about his hairdresser though!

The Führer's eyes are watery, restless, an intense blue. He seems to be glaring angrily at her eyelashes. His manners dazzle her. The way – click! – he keeps – click! – clicking – click! – his glistening calf-length brown boots. A trick flat-footed Charles, away opening a china kangaroo factory in Darwin, ought to be taught. "Veal-comb," the Führer grunts, in a harsh, forced tone, as if his nose was blocked. He draws her attention to six-hundred assembled Bavarian girls dressed in costumes which have a frill of lace around the neck oddly reminiscent of the profile of a newt. One of the maidens steps forward and presents Diana with a posy of stinkweed. The rest break into a lusty folk dance.

Cheering crowds, chanting. *Beguile*, they bellow. *Beguile, beguile.* How she wishes she had brought Plomer and the dictionary with her. Now they are singing some sort of wassail song. Floodlights, fluttering banners, more cheers and chanting. An open Mercedes-Benz takes them along packed streets to the Brown House. The Princess displays a glassy smile. Her bowels are playing her up. It must have been that ham she ate on the plane. The Brown House is just what she needs (although at home, in the old days, they always called it "the little house" or "the smallest room"). The Führer acknowledges the crowds with a funny stiff wave of his arm. "The swastika," he whispers shyly. "Entirely my idea, you know." Goodness! His interest in design surprises and impresses her. Somehow she had not expected it. "Do you have Laura Ashley shops in your country?" she enquires brightly, but Hitler looks away. Perhaps he has not heard her. The car draws up outside a massive building which holds the promise of many flush lavatories. But first she is obliged to ascend to a balcony and admire a swirl of torch-waving members of the League of German Maidens. Such style! The Princess stifles a tiny yawn. It has been a long and tiring day, yet memorable. At her bedside that night she finds a bulse, and next to it a jiffy bag with "To Diana with sincere best wishes, Adolf" written on it. Folding back the little pins she draws out a first edition of *Der Verzweiflungskampf der arischen Volker mit dem Judentum*. What a charming gesture!

At breakfast the Führer has changed into a pair of fetching black leather sans-culottes. His knees are an unexpected blend of pinks and blues, edged by delicate black hairs. He seems moody and out of sorts, silently gazing at the pepper pot and the silver toast rack.

The Princess uses one of her favourite conversational openings. "Vacuum cleaners," she smiles, "have always been immensely important to me. The value of hygiene and cleanliness in everyday life cannot, I think, be too highly stressed."

Her words seem to have an electrifying impact upon the Führer. "But this is incredible!" he ejaculates, displaying perfect English (albeit with a slight Scouse accent). "I, too, believe from the bottom of my heart in purging filth from the world of decent men and women. I myself wash frequently – six or seven times a day." The Führer lowers his voice and adds with a sickly, haunted expression upon his face: "Microbes rush at me, trying to infect me. All the time this goes on! Always, always my dear Diana, beware of bacilli! The powers of darkness stretch out their octopus arms, fasten their sucking cups upon us in a hundred places! We are faced by pestilence, nothing less than the racial tuberculosis of nations! Measures must be taken against the parasites, the eternal leeches, the vampires! The struggle we are waging against the virus is of the same kind as that of Koch and Pasteur! We must cut open the tumours! We must eliminate the termites!"

By the time he has finished the toast is cold. "I feel *exactly* the same way about dirty plates left lying around in the kitchen," she replies, reaching for the thin-cut marmalade. Later she tries some "Good Adolf" canned herring and listens attentively as the Führer explains Horbiger's fascinating world ice theory.

In the afternoon she hosts a reception at the British Embassy. The ambassador, whose name is Eric, has lined up his rosy-cheeked children to greet the Führer. As Hitler enters they stretch out their little arms, raise them and whisper a shy "*Heil*." The Führer seems delighted and clicks his heels. He has come a long way since the days of drawing posters advertising hair tonic and the bed-feathers shop. He barely remembers his efforts to promote Teddy's antiperspirant powder. He moves towards the window, in his mind the dim, curious image of bright blue larger-than-life drops of sweat falling like a stick of bombs from a wrung sock.

"Perhaps later you and our dear Princess might like to play at bumbleputty or take a bummel," interjects Eric, oily and sallow as a kipper. "Or perhaps a short row on the lake for the benefit of the press photographers?"

Hitler shakes his head. "What business would I have in a rowing-boat! I refuse absolutely to row boats, swim or mount a horse. The possible consequences of such activities are intolerable! Time and time again parades go wrong and teach the wise man to avoid horses." He moves away from Ambassador Phipps and begins to devour *Streuselkuchen* after *Streuselkuchen*, *Napfkuchen* after *Napfkuchen*.

The Ambassador slithers after him. "About your restrictions on the import of crab-meat and Welsh bloaters, Führer ..." But Hitler is not listening. He is looking out across the city, admiring the swastikas. Something in the street seems to please him, and he smiles; something in the sky seems to perturb him, and he blanches.

"Few-rrrhhhh," says Diana in a low voice. But Hitler's attention is elsewhere. Suddenly he is screaming, his face drenched in sweat, foam bubbling from all three corners of his mouth.

"See!" he shrieks. "Down there – a bicycle. A glance at nature shows that the bicycle is correctly conceived! But up there, look, an aerostat! A totally insane conception! No one of pure blood could have dreamed of such an abomination! The Jew Issachar Zederblum, alias Lenin, conceived the morass of Bolshevism and now our skies are filled with aerostats! Circumcised Asiatics everywhere are polluting our nation! Read Isaiah 19, 2-3 and Exodus 12, 38. Moses was the first leader of Bolshevism! Mozart wrote the Bible! The aerostat is a floating tumour in the pure sky of German womanhood!"

The Ambassador nods vigorously. "I couldn't agree more, my Führer. You wouldn't catch me travelling in one of those contraptions, I can tell you! I haven't forgotten what happened to poor Nellcock. Have you seen *Kind Hearts and Coronets* yet or are your boffins still having trouble coming up with their time machine? I know there's a League of Nations embargo on uranium exports to Germany but between you, me and that swastika over there I think I could promise one or two boxes – provided of course that you agree to take 300 tons of fish products off our hands. What do you say, Ad, old chap – is it a deal?"

But Hitler has not heard a word. Clenching his fists, trembling, dribbles of saliva still snaking down his chin, his attention is fixed entirely upon the aerostat. The device drifts slowly behind the cathedral and out of sight.

Next day the Princess accompanies the Führer on a hunting expedition. Together they slaughter hundreds of pheasants. Hitler wipes the blood from his Bermuda shorts and takes Diana forcefully by the arm. He gestures at the heaps of dead and dying birds. He chuckles and crunches one under his boot. "Do you know what is in my mind when I see these creatures?" The Princess looks blank. Is it, perhaps, some sort of trick question? The Ambassador, his C.M.G. hanging in the balance, anguish in his eyes, has emphasized to her the importance of humouring the Führer and getting rid of that mountain of rotting crab-meat and bloaters on the quayside at East Kinnock.

"Sandwiches?"

The Führer shakes his head. He seems to be convulsed. He shakes like a sufferer from Parkinson's Disease.

"Jews!" he shrieks, his right eye contracting into a wink. A harsh surge of laughter roars from his throat. It is, the Princess realises, some sort of obscure joke. These Germans! She smiles politely. On their way back to Berlin Hitler is silent once again, a faraway serious look in his brooding blue eyes.

Dead Paraguayans

Almost exactly two years ago, in a field outside Leicester, we came across our first heap of dead Paraguayans. It was a rainy October morning and the traffic was heavy. When we pulled into the lay-by it was because we still had another hundred miles to go and needed a break. But before mother had even taken the Thermos flask out of her wicker basket my sister Angela was saying excitedly, "Something's up. What are those people looking at?"

Ahead of us in the lay-by were a yellow Sierra, a green Peugeot, a scarlet 2CV, a purple Beetle, a white Golf, a red Jaguar, a blue Transit van, a grey Fiesta, a green estate car, a red Sierra towing a caravan, a Polo, an aged Imp, a rotting Minx, an Escort, another Escort, another Sierra, a mini, an Astra, a larger, dirtier Citroën and what if I was not mistaken was a Mazda 323 Fastback with 16 valve, 1.8 litre fuel-injected engine with a 140 bhp thrust that gets a man to 60 mph in 8.6 seconds and with a top speed of 125 mph. The drivers and passengers of these vehicles were grouped at a gap in the hedge, talking and pointing. Two men were looking through binoculars.

Angela ran up to take a look, then came back with a disappointed expression on her face.

"It's only a heap of dead Paraguayans," she said.

"But what are they doing there?" mother asked.

'Decomposing, I think. There are masses and masses of flies and the smell is awful."

'Who wants a sausage and cheese sandwich?" said mother. "There's only two left." But before we had had time to draw lots two police vans drew up. The onlookers gathered by the gap in the hedge were beaten back to their cars by helmeted officers with truncheons. A sergeant came over to our car, rapped on the windscreen with his radio, and said "Hop it. You've got thirty seconds."

Mother put the Thermos back in the basket and we hurriedly drove off.

At the time we thought no more about it but then in December it happened again, this time in a field outside Norwich. There must have been at least two hundred dead Paraguayans, deposited in four layers of fifty. Fearing the police, we did not stop. Next day there was still nothing in the newspapers but even before we had reached York there were signs that an entrepreneurial spirit had sprung up with regard to the matter. All the way up the A1 we kept seeing little hand-painted signs saying DEAD PARAGUAYANS, ONE MILE. TEA, COFFEE, REFRESHMENTS.

"But where do you think they all come from?" mother asked anxiously.

"Paraguay," I said.

They seemed to be everywhere. Stepping out of the Brontë parsonage in Haworth I strolled up the lane and there, heaped against a dry-stone wall, were fifty Paraguayan corpses. Some were in an advanced state of decay but others seemed to be quite fresh. It was much the same at Stonehenge and Stratford-upon-Avon. However, there was nothing in the papers and we thought no more about it until one morning the following March when mother drew back the floral curtains and shrieked like a hedgehog. We ran to see what the matter was. I think we all groaned together. There, close to the gate, completely blocking the drive, was a pile of fifteen dead Paraguayans.

"Why did they have to pick on *us?*" grumbled Nicholas. "Surely the whole point of living in Dumble is to get away from that sort of thing. I shall write to Julian Iron. He'll know what to do."

"I'm surprised there's been nothing on the radio about it."

"And nothing on television either."

Outside, leaves flitted and fluttered across the drive. As drives went it was of a comforting, conventional format. Gravel curved in a crescent, edged by cheerful rhododendrons and dignified privet.

"It's their insolent lack of motion that I find hard to stomach," said Angela. "Not the bluebottles."

"The rolling country of Eastern Paraguay consists largely of igneous formations in which intrusive granite is a common feature," contributed mother. "What's more, steamer communication on the River Paraguay is infrequent, slow, unpunctual and unreliable."

"Those igneous formations contain deposits of copper, lead and other metals, but these are not worked," I added. "The sub-tropical and tropical lowlands of Paraguay are unsuitable for cattle and sheep. Where these animals are found they are liable to be attacked by various diseases."

"Only five hundred tons of the plant *Ilex paraguayensis* were produced in Paraguayan plantations in 1915. The leaves of this plant are used as a substitute for tea," retorted Angela.

"My guess is they are sucked up into the sky by some sort of a reverse plasma vortex, then fall out of the sky when there's an abrupt drop in temperature," said mother, a keen reader of the *Fortean Times*.

"I'm going back to bed," Nicholas yawned. "I'm tired."

"So who's going to move the dead Paraguayans?" muttered father testily. "I was going over this morning to see Giles and show him my new shotgun. I can't possibly get the Range Rover out of the drive until someone does something."

Pah-rah-guh-why, Pah-rah-guh-why, whispered the wind in the branches of our fir trees. Some winds are loquacious, even matey, and seem to have originated in the East End of London, but this was a wind of the better sort, its fine breeding unmistakeable. Born in Kent, it had spent a restless adolescence in Knightsbridge and Chelsea before moving on in middle age to Harrow. The wind's refinement was evident in the way it began to mimic the slow sections of Chopin's Sonata in B Flat minor.

"I will, father," I said, hurrying outside just in time to catch a Beethoven late quartet emanating from the privet. "I'll move the Paraguayans. Where do you want them put?"

Father waved his hands in exasperation. "The village green.

The ditch by the lane. Anywhere."

"Just give me ten minutes." Was that Schubert's Unfinished the wind was finishing-off amid the groaning elms? I tilted my head and tugged at my ears, straining to catch the trill of flutes.

And then it happened. Abruptly, spitefully, the wind broke into "I'm Dreaming of a White Christmas", a nonsensical notion if ever there was one, for I have never known a white Christmas, only grey ones, grim ones, wet ones, dozens, scores, each one swaddled in warm rain and burdened by a floppy dreary miasma of clouds, English clouds, lethargic, shapeless, dull.

The song ended and the wind began to die. There was just a faint, almost inaudible hint (I may have imagined it) of "Smoke Gets in Your Eyes" and then it was gone. Gripping the key tightly in my right hand I hurried across the lawn to the locked shed where father kept his spades and his disinfectant.

Tinctures, Stains, Relics

Yesterday the enormous mirror fell to the floor with a thunderous smash, toppled over on to its face and shattered into fifty-seven pieces.

It had been in our family since the time of my great-grandfather Leo. Can you imagine the sparkle which came to my eyes, the sudden ecstatic acceleration of my pulse, the great clown's grin which twisted my flushed face, the commotion and knockings at the walls of my swollen heart, the acute, quivering rapture, the sharp soft waves of unspeakable pleasure which shot through me, the palsied trembling which shook my limbs as, half-dizzy with the bliss of it all, I hurled myself from the armchair in which I had been dozing, and, ignoring the tiny silver shards popping and hissing beneath my feet, seized the great heavy gold frame and dragged it back into a standing position (or at any rate a half-drunken lean), once more with its back to the wall?

Of course not. How could you?

There are strange kinks and loops in time which few men, blindly reaching out, fingers at full stretch, have the luck to touch (and when touched how nimbly and fish-like they flicker away, vanish!). Most, lost in the diaheliotropism of ordinary life, do not even try. Perhaps if I was to draw your attention to the remarkable parallels with the ecstasy of M. Alphonse Ratisbonne in Rome in 1824 after the sudden disappearance of an entirely black dog – But no. How could you, with your lichen collection and your lovely family, you who live out there in the grey polluted world of mortgage repayments, garden fences, No Entry signs, return tickets, traffic signals, fashion shows, lawn-mowers, ante-natal clinics, secondary schools and twenty-four-hour no waiting restrictions, possibly comprehend the reason why my grin of innocent delight metamorphosed into the radiant smile seen upon a scientist's face when his experiment comes up trumps? How could *you* comprehend the shocking, shimmering possibilities which danced and sang and soared inside my fevered mind – possibilities only half-hinted-at in the crazy colourful jumble of fragments which shone back at me? Any description, however sublime it might be, could be but a profanation of the unspeakable truth. Still, I'll have a bash.

The great flat rectangle was gone forever. No longer would it show the placid, rather colourless interior of a living-room full of dusty old-fashioned I furniture, the big, mute, dominant grandfather clock holding up its black-on-white circular fiction of universal objective time, with, a little way off, yours truly, sufferer from myopia (hence the scowl, the wrinkled brow, the huge tortoiseshell horn-rimmed spectacles wedged upon my scarlet nose), an old man dogged by odd bouts of forgetfulness and in a state of advanced physical decrepitude, dressed in thick green corduroy trousers and a matching flannel waistcoat, sunk in an armchair beneath a picture of Napoleon (oddly resembling the film star Rod Steiger) retreating across a snowbound empty page, next to which: a reproduction water-colour of a windmill and an exquisite aerostat etching by Crunlop, a shelf supporting a large yellowish human skull and a small dark powdery pile of something unidentifiable (moon dust, perhaps), a Welsh dresser nearby bearing its bourgeois freight of floral plates and teacups, next to it my brown bucket of rejection slips, thirty-four numbered cardboard boxes, the fruit bowl piled with oranges and apples and crowned by an impotent solitary mottled banana, the great pastel slice of angel cake which closer inspection would reveal to be shelves of paperbacks neatly filed according to the colour of the spine, one row held up by a large tin globe mysteriously dotted with yellow spots, a three-quarters-open door exposing a fragment of corridor and another door, the door to the bathroom, half-open, revealing a purple mat plus a red enamel mug containing five toothbrushes, and, back in the corridor again, the thin, spectral figure of my wife, lurking (as is only proper for the wife of a writer) where she has always lurked, in the deforming half-light and the shadows, a brown dustpan and brush in her chapped pink hands, while back in the room, beyond the window, a leafless plane tree (must be winter) puts a delicate mesh across a slate-grey distant roof and some rather fluffy, insubstantial clouds.

Instead I found myself gazing at what I at first took to be Pablo Picasso's *Portrait of Ambroise Vollard*. I looked again, and found myself staring at a mutilated Rod Steiger. Steiger frowned, and turned into someone else. I gazed in horrified growing fascination at my own face, horribly altered, with pyramids bulging from brow and scalp. My hands shook and the Picasso vanished, replaced by Leger's *Soldier with Pipe*, in which I could just glimpse myself, dismantled yet still suffering from the red-hot proddings of a lifetime of murderous constipation (not to mention my elephantine piles and brimming boils). Everything began to blur, so that, as I fainted, overwhelmed by emotion and excitement, I caught sight of one final canvas, some sort of post-modernist homage to Cubism and Kurt Schwitters in which the contents of an ash-tray had been tipped across a cascade of dark blood, a vaguely octagonal blotch framed by the bridge of a guitar, an alarm clock, a shard from a cello's end-pin, a fragment of cork tile, the label from a wine bottle, half a playing card (if you must: the Queen of Spades), a bunch of keys, part of a sheet of music with a few bars of *Lillabullero,* a scrap of tapestry showing a blue-green world enclosing a pale stag, a few splinters of faded furniture recently chopped up by a maniac, a postcard of sun-soaked Valladolid, torn fragments of headlines from a newspaper, all dotted with small shattered beads of glass from a multi-coloured dome. It was a first-rate composition which I knew I would never have time to put on canvas in the short time left to me and which, like a sequel to *Hamlet* in the mind of the dying Shakespeare, was soaked up irretrievably by a sudden surge of darkness.

"What's up?" asked Ginny, shaking me out of the sweet misty stupor where my mind roamed joyously free of the shackles of flesh and a linear chronology.

"It's what's *down* that matters!" I rebuked her. I did not

allow my sense of rapture at the mirror's fall to deflect the recognition that she had exceeded her week's quota of questions, something which always puts me in a dangerously volatile mood in which I am capable of almost anything.

Let me explain.

My name is Charles M. Fawkes (none of your business what it stands for). I am a writer and thinker. I am the author of thirty-four important philosophical texts, not a single one of which has seen the light of day. I have been rejected by every single publishing house in the country. The small provincial firm of Gripp & Co once seemed very interested in my seventeenth book, *The General Law of Phantom Bullets and Capitalist Accumulation* but backed out at the very last moment. The Malice Aforethought Press informed me that my *Entombed Toads and Economic Elites* was "excellent" but at 3,250 pages was "just a little too long" and "might well cause our photocopier to overheat". Pffaagh! I have grown weary of the flimsy, excuse-wrapped rejections which have struck my soft, throbbing heart like painfully pointed paper darts from all quarters of the kingdom. Even a letter sent to the local paper about my recent unmistakeable sighting of the planet Vulcan was not published.

Let me make one thing clear: I am not a man who compromises. I made that quite clear to Giacinta on that bright April day I married her, and I make this equally clear to our landlord, Blott, whenever the rascal knocks at our door with one of his familiar wheedling requests for back rent. Blott, like the electricity people and the gas people and the water people and the telephone people and the poll-tax people, wants my money. As I keep telling them, I am like Mozart: I haven't got any. Ginny does her best, but what she earns barely pays for my doughnuts and my A4 refill pads, let alone the walnut-veneer coffin, the small bare plot and the marble headstone I have set my heart on. Since our supply of water, gas and electricity was terminated Ginny has even had to shut down the laundry business which she ran from our bathroom these past thirty years.

The water I now fetch in used quart milk cartons from a nearby park tap. As for warmth and light ... The authorities have clearly underestimated just how long I will be able to hold out with my magnifying glass, my candles and my crate of Laphroaig.

Poor Giacinta. How – like Anna F and Jenny M – she has suffered! She has sacrificed everything a woman desires for the sake of Truth. Presented with a questionnaire which asked him to identify his favourite virtue in a woman, Fort wrote: "Weakness." Precisely my own view! Once, I remember, Giacinta hinted that she wanted children. I immediately became sullen and suspicious. Wasn't I good enough for her? What was the nature of the gap in our relationship that she sought to plug with loud, miniature bipeds? I was obliged to point out to her that only men haunted by a sense of imperfection feel obliged to reproduce themselves (presumably in the hope that the next model will be better than the one before – something any car mechanic or regular purchaser of washing-machines knows to be false). "I," I remember saying, "am haunted in other ways." With a final quotation from Dr Johnson – "a baby is a wet, smelly radio which comes on at full volume in the middle of the night and which you can't switch off" – the matter was disposed of. Every couple of years, whenever pregnancy threatened to cast a shadow over my work, Ginny obligingly made her way to the nearest abortion clinic, finding her way back on public transport by herself and getting on with her laundry work the very next day. She sets a shining example to other women! She is a living testament to faith in the exercise of pure unfettered intellect.

Over the long years of our marriage I have a single image of her: red-cheeked and stout and panting as she beats with a huge wooden spoon at a vast hump of sodden grey clothing rising out of our small foam-filled enamel bath, the very picture of a dinosaur hunter in the Congo who, when all seems lost, finally comes across a stray infant elasmosaurus and at once begins to thrash it into submission. Lately, it is true, she has become much thinner, and glummer, and greyer.

Sometimes it is almost as if she has lost faith in my lifetime's endeavours. I cannot believe this. I refuse to believe it.

Let me explain.

I am haunted in other ways. I am haunted by two far-reaching philosophies which I alone have discovered. Each one, alone, is partial, defective, inadequate. Neither gives the full story. Neither can satisfactorily account for the perplexing, saddening, hilarious, cloudy complexity of modern life. But put the two together ... I have, in short, devoted my whole life to the writings of two of the obscurest men ever to tread the surface of this planet. I, and I alone, have transmuted these baser metals into gold. You can keep your piffling Plato, your pathetic Pascal, your prattling Popper. Give me Fort and Marx any day! Better still, give me Fawkesism.

Let me explain.

Charles Fort was born in Germany in 1818 but spent most of his life abroad. In his later years he lived in London, where he died on 10 March 1883. He wrote many non-fiction books and pamphlets on a wide range of subjects, few of which were successful and which are now virtually unknown. Perhaps Fort's most ambitious book was *Capital,* a huge, unfinished three-volume study of capitalist society.

Karl Marx was separated from Fort by only the tiniest kink in time. He was born in Albany, New York, in 1874 and died in London on 3 May 1932. His best work, *The Book of the Damned,* a study of unexplained phenomena, was published by Boni and Liveright in 1919.

Modesty forbids it, but an historian's sense of objectivity over-rules her and insists that I add:

Charles M. Fawkes was born in Penge in 1933 and will die in Bloomsbury next Tuesday. His best book, *Frog Showers and the End of Imperialism,* is a massive eight-volume study of the relationship between the slump-boom cycle and visitations from the sky. As yet unpublished, it is available for inspection upon application to the author's widow. Ask to see Box 17. Fawkes is the originator of "Fawkesism", a wholly new way of looking at things.

You have never heard of either Fort or Marx or Fawkesism? I am not surprised. In the course of my researches I have learned that Fort's *Capital* was a tremendous influence upon a long-forgotten group of Russian revolutionists. One, Vladimir Ilyich Lenin, devoted his entire life to Fort's teachings. After his premature death his sister Anna wrote: "I can see him as if it were yesterday sitting on a kitchen stove covered with newspapers and making violent gestures, as he spoke of the new horizons which opened out to anyone who followed Fort's theories."

I have the impression Lenin might conceivably have written something of real worth had he not been knocked off his bicycle and killed by a motorist near Juvisy-sur-Orge in the autumn of 1909. Another devotee of Fort's work was Trotsky, a long forgotten Russian exile who was captured in Petrograd by the Provisional Government and killed in ambiguous circumstances at the end of August 1917, after the successful coup by General Kornilov. (There is even a story that Vladimir, son of V. D. Nabokov – the Minister killed in the bungled assassination attempt on Prime Minister Miliukov in March 1922 – had a hand in the killing, but it must be said that this seems unlikely. Nabokov Junior, a minor comic novelist, cannot help us here: he died in May 1940 when the *Champlain* was torpedoed off the French coast by a German submarine.)

Marx, by comparison, has had no influence at all upon anyone except perhaps myself. By all accounts he was a short, plump, merry little man with a walrus moustache and a loud, booming laugh. His important years were spent in a flat near King's Cross station, accumulating press cuttings about paranormal happenings. A single surviving photograph shows him slumped in a rocking chair, behind which, on the wall, can be seen framed specimens of outsize spiders, a photograph of a cricket ball beside a giant hailstone, an autographed snapshot of his favourite movie actress, Lillian Gish, and a small shelf bearing his treasured heap of something said to resemble dirty asbestos, which once fell inexplicably out of the sky and landed at his feet in Russell Square.

Charles Fort ... Karl Marx ... Charles Fawkes. *The Augurers* – that is how I like to think of them. Don't you find the similarity of the names uncanny? That is not the only resemblance which haunts me. I am rather overweight, and so were they. I have facial hair (a beard, if you must know) and so had they. They lived in central London, and went each day to the reading room of the British Museum to do their researches, and so do I. They were (inexplicably) failures, and so (inexplicably) am I.

The only gap in my vast researches concerns doughnuts and toothbrushes. There seems to be no surviving evidence that either Marx or Fort were gluttons for doughnuts, but in view of my own mountainous consumption (I get through 26 dough-nuts a day, with an extra dollop of strawberry jam and a generous sprinkling of caster sugar on top) I feel in my guts that they were. I also feel fairly certain that they, too, must have shared my deep-seated belief that a toothbrush should only be used at most for 48 hours, before lying fallow for five days. This ensures that dangerous microbes are given time to die off.

Fort's grave in tangled Highgate I excavated in a moment of heady inspiration after Giacinta dragged me off to the Empire to see *Intruder in the Dust*. I lugged away his skull in a sack, reckoning that no one else in the world but me could possibly want it, or would grant it the prominence and respect it deserved. I did it one night in 1956, in the same week that my beard was wrenched off in the great hurricane of that year. This caused Giacinta to comment many years later that in appearance and behaviour I bore a startling resemblance to the rat catcher in Truffaut's *Une Belle Fille Comme Moi,* a film I have never seen. How I abhor gratuitous allusion!

Now perhaps you begin to cross the golden brink of understanding. Fawkesism is the science of the laws of motion of capitalism and cosmic oddity. Bankruptcy, recession and frog-falls in Felixstowe are all one to me. Fawkesism proph-ecies the end of our world and the birth of another. What's more, the end is near. I feel it, sense it. I can almost smell it. I can read the signs as well as any shaking seismologist, smirking sociologist or so-sure Saussurian. Hence my rapture.

In 1911, Norwegian troops led by Amundsen reached the South Pole; in 1977 the United States of Supreme America (U.S.S.A.) invaded Exicom, Erup, Zualaveen, Libraz, Vialiob, Liche, Antigenar, Dangera and Guanicaar, installing puppet regimes and reducing millions to squalor, terror and horrific suffering. The fight-back is continuing and the end is near. Day after day there are remote far-off thuddings and booms as another bomb goes off. Sometimes thick black pillars of smoke can be seen slowly crawling across the reddish apocalyptic evening sky. Day after day jet fighters pass in screaming pairs low over the city, making the whole flat shake. The newspapers are full of troubles and shocks. A ghost has been seen in Cock Lane. Angels have been observed over Mons by numerous sound military eyewitnesses. They were frantically strumming their harps and protesting about E.E.C. agricultural policy. A week earlier the Loch Ness monster was seen to rise out of the loch near Foyers, give a nervous shudder, turn pale and plunge back into the depths. Meanwhile the streets are piled high with rotting sacks, wasps crawling everywhere across the spilt potato peelings and the empty passion-fruit yogurt pots. The pavements are thick with animal excreta and broken glass. Small clouds of flies jig and dance at every street corner, celebrating the popularity of the Conservative Party and their unbelievable good fortune at the prospect of unending right-wing government. The other night, returning home from the reading room, I came across half-a-dozen cockroaches holding a round-table discussion on the doorstep. I would not be at all surprised to learn that they had recently plummeted from the sky, direct from Vulcan. Some were for Theever, some for Nellcock, but all were plump and sleek and very pleased with the state of things.

Yes, the end is near, so near. Last week the annual carnival procession passed by with the usual paper dragon and shivering, moronically grinning carnival queen. But something went wrong, there was a sudden charge by the riot police, the carnival queen had her face split in two, the night ended in screams and sirens, breaking windows, mass arrests, the unearthly unending flickering whirl of blue light, the primitive thumping of shields.

As the poet said, things flip and flop apart. Even Ginny is not immune from the growing madness. Yesterday, when I enquired somewhat testily what had happened to my 11am plate of jam doughnuts and pot of Earl Grey she snapped, "Get them yourself!" Get them myself, can you believe? I begin to wonder if there is not more in *Invasion of the Body Snatchers* than meets the eye. Has Ginny's body been surreptitiously colonised by a hideous alien species? Was it the real Ginny who refused to fry me eggs for breakfast or was it an automaton lacking all human feeling?

Ginny has even gone so far as to suggest that great-grandfather's mirror fell off the wall because the pin had been loosened by the wall having been shaken each time the jets fly overhead. What a preposterous notion! It is as if she has forgotten what I told her about the last days of Marx. It is, incredibly, almost as if she no longer believes in Fawkesism. I cannot believe this. I refuse to believe it. I have devoted a lifetime to an in-depth study of capitalist economics and the paranormal, and I am not quitting now. Everything that is happening in the world today – the red-eyed terrier in East Grinstead which vanished in a puff of green smoke, the collapse of the British economy, the orange UFO seen over Bognor pier, the devaluation of the dollar – convinces me that I am right. Soon everything will go dark, and while the world gives a Munch-like shriek of bewilderment and fear I will be sitting here, understanding everything, giving a modest chuckle of satisfaction. Or perhaps everything will end in a white, blinding flash. I have never forgotten that time I fainted in Africa. One moment I was standing in the street, in the furnace of the noon-day sun, the next everything I was looking at – some palm trees, a passing truckload of soldiers, a picturesque one-legged beggar – ebbed terrifyingly from view. For a fraction of a second I found myself staring at a white void. "I've gone blind!" I gasped, before losing consciousness and pitching forwards across the dusty sidewalk. A few seconds later, of course, I came to, to find that reality had quickly reassembled itself and that the beggar was pawing at my safari suit, his beery-breath washing over me as he gabbled for coins.

This time when the world goes white, that will be it. There will be no re-assembly, except, *peut-être*, many years later, when a tiny handful of deformed, half-mutated survivors will eke out in caves a miserable existence. I can see exactly how it will be. After their lentils and their raw, mildly radioactive rat steak they will pass from hand to hand the precious, priceless original manuscripts of Fawkesism. In a thousand years' time, when printing has been re-invented, I will be world famous. They will say I was a guy who lived up to his name.

Meantime I must settle for obscurity in Bloomsbury. Fort, who spent much of his life denouncing long-forgotten economists as addled and deluded Don Quixotes, came to feel in his last years that the Don was in fact rather like *himself*: "Sleepless, without appetite, coughing badly, a little perplexed, and not without occasional bouts of a profound melancholia ..." And as Marx wryly remarked of his penultimate book, *Lo!*: "Maybe it's awful. Maybe somebody had to do it. Maybe it was just my luck to be picked out."

The hands of the clock maintain their remorseless motion, day plunges towards night. It is time to leave the kitchen where I have been fumbling and failing to make myself a cup of tea (what is to be done with those black brittle leaves? and how *does* a kettle work?). I glide along the dark corridor and enter this little room. It was always my favourite room. The reading I have done here! The thinking! The notes I have jotted while waiting, waiting, waiting!

Charles Fort ... Karl Marx ... Charles Fawkes. Think of them as the Holy Trinity of modern philosophy. Think of Fawkesism as the destiny of a grotesque, absurd, darkly disintegrating, mad, unequal world.

I close the door behind me and bolt it against intruders. Then, shielding my eyes against the yellow glare of frosted glass, I open the window. Down below, in the miserable deep-in-shadows backyard, I can see Ginny. She must be doing her spring cleaning, for I can see her burning a mound of old cardboard boxes, doubtless full of rubbish. On her face there is a radiant smile of fulfilment. I am glad to see she has cheered up. Later, I suspect, she will come to me with a hangdog face and a plate of doughnuts and tell me she has been a very silly girl.

A rush of smoke and crumbly ticking blackened paper obliges me to shut the window again. I retire (wonder what she's burning?) to my favourite seat. Ahead of me, on the bright creamy door, the shadow of five toothbrushes in a white enamel mug holds up a cautionary skeletal hand against shallow pleasures and the laxity induced by sunshine. I think once more of great-grandfather's broken mirror and of the last days of Marx.

Great-grandfather had a beard like Fort's and spent much of his life exploring Russia. Apart from the mirror he bequeathed an estate of 2,000 acres, a sled and a rather worn wolf-skin rug. He died at Waterloo, of exposure, in a bleak sub-zero December. They found him in the waiting room, bolt upright, an angry glare in his glassy eyes, doomed never to hear the approaching friendly rattle of the 9.10 to Dorking (it had been delayed by a points failure).

For Fort and Marx the end was even slower. Edmund Wilson's *To Astonishing Fin Land* (a study of financial sharks in the U.S.S.A.) gives a touching picture of Fort's death at his desk. As for Marx ...

The poignant final pages of Marx's diary for 1932 read as follows:

Feb. 13 I have been half dead – so weak couldn't go out walking.

Feb. 19 Am sleeping poorly, have cut down on beer.

Feb. 20 Finished *Wild Talents* today. Jenny came to me & said: "Did you hear that?" "No." "Not the loud crash?" Later while at dinner 2 packages of sugar fell.

Feb. 26 New difficulty in shaving – gaunt places in my face.

On the morning of 3 May Marx was taken by ambulance to

the Royal Hospital. Advance copies of *Wild Talents* were brought, but he could not lift his hand to take them. He died that day.

There is something else I have not mentioned. I was born on 3 February 1933 – exactly nine months from the day of Marx's death. Once I regarded the idea of reincarnation as utter claptrap, the last resort of fat, moustachio'd middle-aged women anxious to fill the void of their dull, semi-educated suburban lives with the consoling illusion that in a previous era they wore scanty clothing and lived an erotic, exotic life as Cleopatra, Queen of Egypt. Now I am not so sure. Upon reflection it seems to me highly probable that at the moment of Marx's death some sort of metaphysical spark crossed from his expiring mind into my mother's womb. You will, I think, appreciate that I do not wish to probe too far into the delicate biological details of the matter. Let me simply say that the concept of the homunculus has in my opinion been far too easily dismissed by modern science.

What's that? *You still* do not quite comprehend the significance of that broken mirror?

Let me spell it out so that even a child of three could understand.

One evening in March 1924 Marx was reading when he heard a thump. A picture had fallen off the wall in the next room. His wife reminded him that two pictures had recently fallen in the flat above. Six days later Marx heard the crash of glass and discovered that another picture had fallen from the wall. "It was so sharp and loud that for hours afterwards I had a sense of alertness to dodge missiles. It was so loud that Mrs C upstairs heard it," he wrote.

Ten days went by. On the morning of 28 March Marx discovered a second picture had fallen in the same room as the previous one. It had fallen from a place about a metre above the bureau upon which he kept his boxes of notes. Among these notes were accounts of pictures unaccountably felling from walls!

In October of that year Marx was in the front room thinking

96

casually of pictures which fell from walls. He was staring right at a picture above the corner of the bureau where he stored his notes. What happened next does not need to be described, and so I shall not describe it. Suffice to say that exactly five years later Marx was discussing these very matters *when a pan fell from a pile of utensils in a nearby closet.*

The end is near, I sense it more than ever. It is almost as if I was a creature in somebody's short story. I sense the author's impatience. He's bored with me, wants to be rid of me. He's frowning at the screen, scowling at his keyboard. Any moment now he'll press Q for QUIT and have done with me. Nonsense, can't be true. I refuse to believe it.

In a moment of naked doubt Marx once remarked of his books that each one was perhaps merely "a sanitarium for over-worked coincidences". I, thankfully, have never suffered from the slightest twinge of doubt about the importance of my work. I am free – yes, FREE and waiting for a sign. A sign! I half expect to hear another sudden convulsive thud and smash as the small circular bathroom mirror slips from its hook. It would be good to have my certainties punctuated like that. Or perhaps there will be darkness, perhaps a blinding whiteness.

I cannot say. All I know is that something – the end of the world? a paranormal happening? a stock exchange collapse of epic proportions? a new and astonishing perception that will throw my life into final perspective? – is about to happen. I know that, as I sit here, waiting, my green corduroy trousers curled around my ankles, clenching my teeth and with an heroic religious grimace upon my flushed, shining face, *something,* something powerful and immense, something devastatingly final, is on the brink of explosive birth.

The Bloating of Nellcock

> towards me did run
> A thing more strange than on Nile's slime the sun
> E'er bred ...
>
> John Donne, *Satire 4*

> ...episodes of this sort, which at first sight seem to be amusing and indecent curiosities ...
>
> Leon Trotsky, *Kuda Idet Angliya?*

1

His childhood. He was born – But let's skip the strange intercourse of sweating, watchful toad with crafty weasel, the enigmatic alchemies of yellowish amphibian's froth and glaucous faeces, the peculiar movements of something out there, beginning to wriggle, quickening into life upon a mud bank, made sulphurous by the sun, chilled by the moon, the original, the one and only Nellcock.

Let us simply say that he was not the first homunculus to emerge out of the vast seaweed-strewn wastes of the Nurrud estuary in Dyfed. Just as you would go to Wiltshire to see a crop circle or to Inverness-shire to encounter a plesiosaur, so, picnicking innocently by the Nurrud one bright April morning long ago, you would not have been especially surprised to see Nellcock's tiny figure coming ashore. Even then, though mystified at what had happened, understanding nothing of his situation, he still managed to dilate and contract at will, and repeatedly, the small oblong aperture situated at the top of his windpipe. And so, still trying out the tones of his voice – one moment a warm, whirring Nurrud brogue, the next a piping Welsh whine, now the poignant twang of public reminiscence, then a matey drawl – his little toes made their first poignant contact with dry land, that realm where destiny waited. The next instant his tiny, fiery red eyes sighted a tub abandoned at the roadside. Although it was an old tub, and rather dirty, instinct made him sprint towards it. He began (it was an historic moment) to thump it.

At the age of six his future as a deipnosophist seemed certain. Guzzling filched apples, he loved to prattle. Hogging the pie, he invariably piped up and rattled on. Devouring fried eggs and beans, he became voluble, prolix. At puberty he used to perorate under the sheets. One day he became lost in a welter of subordinate clauses and did not return until dusk, panting and red-faced. At sixteen he loved nothing better than to rise to speak, ejaculating in full view of passers-by. How he spouted, shuddering! How he loved to stand on stumps, tuning his rant, oblivious to the pain of the amputees.

Not everyone was sure about Nellcock. A wise old woman prophesied that he would be prone to venery by reason of wind. She did not live to see whether her prophecy would come true. The following day, en route to an appointment at the optician's, she was on the top deck of the Swansea bus, puffing on her pipe and chuckling over Lenin's treatment of the renegade Kautsky in her Chinese edition of *Imperialism, the Highest Stage of Capitalism*, when a wheel came off. Her name was Hattie. The bus plunged into a gorge, killing fifteen. Nellcock heard the grown-ups discussing the disaster next day. He shrugged. He was more interested in his magic egg. Many years later, a famous figure, he became adept at feigning shock and sorrow at news of earthquakes, train crashes, bomb outrages, deranged meteorites manipulated by left-wing agitators, unruly prickles lobbed by Irish louts, drunken Italian rabbits, and foul-mouthed militant thistles, all of which secretly delighted him, facilitating, as they did, the opportunity for public use of his larynx. Only for exploding gas mains did he truly grieve.

The magic egg had been a gift from Hattie, given the day before she boarded the doomed omnibus. Although she did not find Nellcock an attractive child, she was prepared to give him the benefit of the doubt – provided, of course, that he gave no evidence of being a social-chauvinist or sought to deny the possibility of national liberation wars in the imperialist epoch. Nellcock rewarded her with warbled denials, an ingratiating smile, and some hollow words of thanks.

2

His appearance. He emerged from the deiparous estuary mud with bedded hair standing on end, beetroot-cheeked, hooped in flab, this paunch big with a spare pair of lungs. His locomotive powers were much the same as an ordinary person's, except for that powerful muscular tug to the right, which as a young man he corrected in the traditional manner of all Welsh homunculi by feigning an extravagant lean to the left. This posture served him well until it was no longer important.

What did Nellcock really consist of, apart from empty words and wind? This question has never been authoritatively answered. As the only person to witness his birth (I was on a nearby hilltop with a pair of X7 binoculars and a butterfly net, maintaining a lonely vigil for strange phenomena) let me place on record, for the very first time, the facts. Nellcock consisted of skin, fat, flesh, veins, arteries, ligaments, glands, genitals, humours and articulations. He was an invertebrate but not an inebriate. His brain was about the size of a centipede's, and like the centipede he was capable of adopting many different positions in order to escape from difficult situations. His meseraic veins became obstructed when he was forty, as a consequence of which the passage of the chilus to the liver was corrupted, and turned into rumbling and wind. His head was exactly the shape of a child's building block, but bigger. The shape of his head determined the following two behavioural traits: (i) when faced by a line chalked on the ground he would always halt and prostrate himself; (ii) when afflicted by toothache he avoided dentists and sought a cure in the incantations of a witch whose charges were very reasonable.

There was a sly, vindictive expression on his face the day he removed the wheelnuts from the floor of the garage, when Quelch's back was turned. Quelch was the mechanic at the bus depot. He was distantly related to Hattie, who only the year before had given young Nellcock a conjuring set. MERLIN'S BOX OF WONDERS contained three plastic cups, four small fluffy balls, a pack of marked cards for observing with the aid of "Merlin's magic spectacles" (which were plastic and pink) and a white wand. They inspired in the boy a lifelong interest in sleight-of-hand, deception, circumvention, meretricious- ness, guile, insubstantiality, cozenage, pettifoggery, wiles, ruses, feints, dodges, diversions, legerdemain, ventriloquism, tokenism, simulacra, mummery and imposture, together with an appetite for audiences, whom he loved to dupe, gull, man- ipulate, bamboozle, string along, cajole, lull, soothe, flatter, inveigle and shanghai in a shameless, barefaced manner crammed with false pleas, evasions, concoctions, and make- believe.

"Strange," thought Quelch. "What on earth has happened to those wheelnuts?"

He groped beneath the Cardiff coach, something he loathed. In his heart of hearts Quelch did not wish to go through life dressed in filthy overalls, with grease on his cheeks and oil- stains on his socks. Each morning as he opened up his box of spanners, he remembered what Nietzsche once said: "A philosopher is a man who never ceases to experience, see, hear, suspect, hope, and dream extraordinary things ..." Quelch was sick of gaskets and pistons and big-ends. He was sick of Wales. When the time was right he planned to leave for Uruguay. There he would make a clearing in the primeval forest, build himself a cabin, grow lettuce, and really get to grips with epistemology, astrophysics and constitutional theory.

In the pungent darkness his fingers vainly raked the coarse sticky surface of the depot floor.

"That you, Quelch?" said a voice.

"Yes," said Quelch, cracking his head on the exhaust pipe. Quelch paused to wonder whether or not the dull, metallic, reverberating sound in his ears was that of the exhaust pipe vibrating or an intriguing aural illusion stemming, perhaps, from a mild concussion.

"It's me, Squibb," said Eck. Eck was a sallow hulk who liked kidding. He had many missing teeth and was especially interested in mountaineering, boxing, developments in Marxist theory and candy floss. "I saw your ankles and thought I recognised the stains. Have you seen Nellcock? I have something for him."

"He was in here earlier. He said he was looking for you. He'd heard of your interest in carburettors."

"That wasn't why I wanted to see him. Hattie told me she'd lent him her copy *of Imperialism, the Highest Stage of Capitalism.* Apparently he wanted it for a vanishing trick. He's a clever lad and no mistake. Hattie says he dresses up in a socialist agitator's red cloak and a working-class cloth cap, throws her book over his left shoulder, waves his wand, takes two steps to the right, and – hey presto! The cloak and the cap have disappeared and in its place you see a moderate's yellow waistcoat, a realist's dark tie and a pragmatist's navy-blue blazer."

"I've seen it done before. Lots of times."

"Ah, well. The lad still has a long way to go. Anyway, the problem is I'm supposed to be giving a talk tonight at the Institute. Next week someone's coming to talk about the Aleppo Button, and I need to put up a good show. I was thinking it was high time I gave the lads a popular outline of imperialism touching on finance capital, the export of capital and the division of the world among capitalist combines. I need to bone up on the way in which the export of capital abroad becomes a means for encouraging the export of commodities. I'm a bit rusty in that quarter."

"Sorry, can't help you there. I'm looking for some wheelnuts."

Quelch wriggled out. "Eck! But I thought – ".

Eck grinned and departed.

"The Swansea bus! It's gone! And the wheelnuts aren't on the nearside front wheel!"

Quelch threw down his spanner and at once ran to his lodgings in the next village. He raced upstairs to his room and began hurriedly thumbing through Parmenides and Heraclitus for tips on what to do next.

3

His biography. This is not the first, far from it. Soon after Nellcock attained high office the first one appeared, by Dunlop. Then there was a shoddy paperback by Gland, a substantial tome by Croup, and a two volume study by Michelin. Hagiographies, all. Can you believe that not one of them mentions Hattie, or the wheelnuts? Not one of these writers has managed to spot the witty, unmistakeable allusion to Nellcock ("the bloat king") in *Hamlet*, III, iv, 183.

Mine is not yet completed. It will end, next Saturday, with the puncturing of Nellcock, his expiry, and the sound emitted as he diminishes, a sound which I fully expect to resemble a garrulous gasp, followed by a piggy squeal, and then an indecent squirt, a whoosh, and finally a plangent whinge, in E flat.

4

His favourite food. The bloater, naturally. What precisely is a bloater? This is the sort of question Quelch adored. "There are two kinds of knowledge," he'd say, clenching his monkeywrench and throbbing. "There is KNOWLEDGE OF FACT and there is KNOWLEDGE OF THE CONSEQUENCE OF ONE AFFIRMATION TO ANOTHER." The bloater illustrates this better than pylons or castanets. "Bloater" is found between "blitzkrieg", which has one meaning, and "blob", which has four or five.

"Blitzkrieg" is a barren, one-dimensional word, redolent of caterpillar tracks, and boots, and helmets passing through holes in hedges. "Blob", by contrast, is not fascist but fecund and fun-filled. There is a movie called *The Blob*, which perhaps you too have seen, a long long time ago. Perhaps, when

Nellcock has been dealt with, we can run off to Cromer, and live under assumed names in one of those little bungalows along the fast crumbling cliff, and grow old together, chuckling over the faded, unreal, possibly unreliable memory of the blob cornered in the supermarket aisle, if it is truly possible to corner a blob, which in real life, outside the needs of a Hollywood story line, I doubt. "Blob" means "a blot" or "a round drop" or "a nought" or "a spot of colour" or "a drop of liquid" or "a small roundish mass" or "an alien life form sometimes found in North American desert communities". Between blitzkrieg and blob lies the bloater, a humble herring dried with smoke. Nellcock (and here I must point out that, though my options are open, I personally favour delaceration) ate his first bloater on the day he was elected to Parliament. He sank his slightly decayed teeth into the butter-sodden tangy tingling texture. Later, occupying high office, he habitually gorged himself on bloater paste sandwiches while travelling to and fro in a shiny black limousine. His adoration of the bloater became a part of his public image, like his ginger freckles, his interest in throat pastilles, his profound rapport with dogs, nurses, jelly babies and shrimps, and his fine taste in classical music. But not even his closest aides ever thought to ask if all that butter was good for him.

5

His assassination. When did I first decide to exterminate Nellcock? Was it the wet November night I stayed home and watched *The Manchurian Candidate* on television? Was it the hot afternoon I crushed six wasps with a rolled-up copy of *The Times Literary Supplement*? In my childhood I remember watching Tim next door tear open a penny banger and empty the powder upon a chrysalis, then toss on a lighted match and screech with pleasure (Tim is now Under Secretary of State for Employment). Was it then that I first came to be interested in pest control? Or was it the unexpected ending of *The Parallax View* which gave me the idea? I am not sure.

His bloating. It began slowly, then accelerated. To bloat is to cause to swell. It is to puff up. It is to make vain. Fast speaking is a consequence of abundance of wind, the inescapable consequence of bloating. To bloat is to grow turgid, to dilate. Nellcock took on a slippery marine air. He spoke rapidly, with a pronounced delacrymation. Soon he would have no further use for limousines or sofas. He was evolving back to the salt sea. He was becoming soft and bald and glistening. I decided that a lightweight one-man harpoon would be just the ticket. For-tunately I am an extraordinarily tall person, so there was no problem concealing it under my trench coat. I read in the newspapers that Nellcock had been invited back to Dyfed to unveil the Kautsky memorial at three o'clock. After harpooning Nellcock I planned to sink to my knees, discard my coat, rub myself in vanishing cream and crawl among the confusion of ankles, chanting in a Glaswegian accent, "Kautsky's theoretical critique of imperialism has nothing in common with Marxism and serves only as a preamble to peace and unity with the opportunists and social-chauvinists, precisely for the reason that it evades and obscures the very profound and funda-mental contradictions of imperialism!" I was confident such a strategy would deflect suspicion, but just in case it failed and I had to resort to brute force I packed eight copies of *Moby-Dick,* a novel which I have always found invaluable in brawls, riots and civil wars. As things turned out Nellcock travelled to Dyfed by aerostat, with fifty-seven supporters. Just before his ascent he gave a short speech to an assembly of baggage hand-lers, reporters and pug-owners in which he called for greater state investment in the bloater industry. "Let me say one thing," said Nellcock. "Let me say unequivocally, and unilater-ally, and unrelentingly, and unambiguously, and unendingly, that there is, and was, and will be, and should be, and must be – ".

Only after the wicker gate had been shut and the aerostat had faded from sight was it discovered that the batteries in everyone's equipment had gone flat. Since none of the reporters present had actually listened to more than Nellcock's first thirty-one words (which they had heard on innumerable previous occasions) his last public speech cannot confidently be reconstructed, although a pug-owner named Dolly swore she had woken up and heard something about the need for greater state investment in bloaters.

If it had not been for the scarlet bloater on the aerostat's side I do not think I would have made the connection as I sheltered on the dry side of the bus-disaster cross on the bleak rain-swept hillside. Blobs of rain clung to the crumbling names engraved on the base of the monument and suddenly there it was, looming out of the clouds. A huge fish was painted along the ribs of the vast craft. Almost by instinct, hoping against hope that it was not a red herring, I raised the harpoon and fired. There was a soft explosion, followed by a tremendous hiss. The aerostat shuddered, and shot off erratically back in the direction of Japan. The basket tilted abruptly, and a plump, unmistakeable figure toppled out.

Nellcock drifted gently downwards, as if in slow motion. The absence of bone structure, the size of his brain and the wind resistance created by his massive girth all helped to put a brake on his descent. He did not fall vertically, but in a slow, deliberate trajectory to the right. As he fell, he gabbled. A stream of inaudible subordinate clauses fluttered from his rear. For a moment a gap opened up in the storm and the sun came out, and there, three hundred miles distant, I saw the noble architecture of the House of Lords. Nellcock saw it too, and began to flap his arms vigorously, as if hoping to make it that far.

Perhaps the harpoon had caught him a glancing blow and pierced his skin. All I know is that suddenly Nellcock seemed to get smaller and smaller and was no longer drifting but falling at great speed. By an uncanny coincidence he landed in the Nurrud estuary, at the exact spot from which he had emerged forty-nine years earlier. At the point of impact there was a sudden eruption of muck, followed by the foul stench of putrefaction and liberated gases. Nellcock was never seen again. The aerostat and the fifty-seven supporters made an emergency landing in a wheat field outside Cardiff (leaving a ball of crushed wheat which three weeks later was hailed as the first Welsh crop circle). The government held a trained Irish seagull with a sharp beak responsible. Holding my nose, I made my way down the hillside and hurled the harpoon into a deep dark pool beneath a massive waterfall. Then I hurried home to complete the final page of my book.

7

His magic egg. For many years it was on display in the Museum of Class Traitors outside Bawdy (parking, buffet facilities, no pugs or bulldogs please). By this time the egg had taken on the appearance of a small withered object the size of a rat dropping. Beside it in the glass cage were the instructions, translated from the Mandarin by the Dutch importer:

(i) Put the little creature into water, see what kind of strange creature it will become? After one hour it will swell out and grow thirty to fifty times in a single day.

(ii) It grew in size after one day but see! Ho prester! It shrinks to its original size gradually when you take it from water. If you want to play again just put it back to water and it will swell out as before.

(iii) Do not put into your mouth, though it is not harmful to bodies. Do not transport by aerostat. Keep it carefully please!

The egg was lost, along with everything else, in the great Dyfed earthquake. By that time Eck had long since left for the Cordilleras, where he suffered greatly from toothache. Quelch took up skin-diving but stayed well away from waterfalls. Then he developed a strange aversion to water and became a familiar figure along the beaches of St Bride's Bay, shaking his fist at the sea and abusing Heidegger. The local Job Centre, hearing that he wished to live and work amid sand, loaned him a child's spade and sent him to Morar. The rain drove him away. Quelch is now in Egypt, helping to repair the Sphinx. The end.

To the Wormshow

My earliest memory? Shooting through space at immense speed, smacking into sponge and jelly, crawling a short distance in the darkness perhaps, miraculously unhurt. Barely time to get my breath back before suffering the gross, shapeless, slippery embrace of a creature from some far planet with (so I imagine) a different climate, a different gravitational pull ... Days, perhaps weeks passed. I was a prisoner. I remember (I think I remember) trying to escape. In parts of Cornwall, among the vast, rain-swept granite droppings of long-vanished giants, small openings are sometimes found where rocks have tumbled across each other. It is commonly believed that anyone afflicted by rheumatism or lumbago will be cured if such an opening is entered, and the low, narrow passageway traversed, and the sufferer emerges from the grey, hope-filled fragment of light at the far end. Perhaps I am of Cornish ancestry, or perhaps simply born of a long line of lumbago sufferers – and without question cursed by piles, boils, dry flaking skin, freckles and an hereditary speech impediment – for I remember (I am almost sure I remember) trying to squeeze my way out between the dark, damp, curving walls of my prison.

Later, when I realised there was no escaping simply by my own unaided efforts, I adopted a squatting position. With my fists up against my face, boxer-style, ready to ward off the blows which I feared would rain down upon me when least expected, I thought of St Jerome in his cool lonely cave. I endeavoured to imitate his admirable posture of apparent detached philosophical meditation. Perhaps to avoid showing their faces, my jailors had resorted to sending me my food by means of a tube resembling a piece of old hose pipe. What they passed along it was unimaginative and monotonous – a sort of soupy slop, quite devoid of texture, flavour or primary colours.

Since my release some parts of the ordeal, thankfully, have

been blotted from my mind. The lack of fibre in my diet, I suspect, was deliberate, resulting in bodily wastes which were never more than a pale, watery liquid and for which, in retrospect (though my gorge rises at the very thought of it), there was only one medium of disposal.

The small windowless unlit room in which I was kept prisoner seemed to be in close proximity to a mill or factory. There was a persistent, tumultuous THUMP!-THUMP!-THUMP! which went on unceasingly, and which at times was the romantic churn of an old foaming water wheel in some fast deep rural stream bordered by weeping willows, among the branches of which brightly plumaged finches chattered and played, but which more often than not was the dull mechanical thudding of machinery beside a conveyor belt along which armoured car chassis after armoured car chassis slowly moved, attended by a swarm of workers, all wearing goggles.

After some weeks my hearing seemed to sharpen. The THUMP!-THUMP!-THUMP! went on all day and all night – not that I, plunged in utter darkness, was capable of distinguishing them apart – but in time I began to detect other sounds, beyond that rhythmic din. The presence of defective plumbing systems became apparent, making odd rushing noises, squeaks and gurgles, and strange reverberating rattles redolent of a lavatory being flushed on the floor above, or a bath next door clearing its throat, resulting in blockages, trapped pockets of air, palsied shudderings climaxing in sudden liberating explosions, familiar enough I dare say to those luckless enough to occupy low rent multi-occupant properties in dubious neighbourhoods, but which at the time caused me, in my innocence and ignorance, not a little distress.

In prison memoirs you will always find energetic and vigorous personages who, denied their pocket watches and wholly deprived of light, swiftly devise an accurate method of recording the passing of the days and who, though plunged in abyssal gloom, surrounded by mildew and with only a spider for company, are able, when asked the time, confidently to assert that it is a quarter to four in the afternoon, and that the day is the second Tuesday in September. Such prisoners, unbroken by fate, their brains buzzing with chess teasers, old remembered crossword puzzles of astonishing difficulty, and fresh thoughts about metaphysics, language and ideology, invariably learn two foreign languages while in confinement, besides walking six miles a day in a space of two square metres, reconstructing through memory *The Adventures of Don Quix-ote,* managing two hundred press-ups each day to keep fit and occasionally performing anarchic handstands in order to escape the dangerous enchantments of total symmetry. I was not like that. Much of the time I lay curled up, in a sort of grey half-sleep, bored and apathetic and putting on weight.

It must have been after about six months (although it might have been after only a couple of hours) that I first heard voices. Voices! At first they seemed far away, muffled, indecipherable. In time they grew more distinctive and I was able to tell that they were the voices of a man and a woman. Before long I was able to identify scraps of language. At first the words were dulled and blurred ("MIST-AIR-HAT-LIE" the woman kept saying, incomprehensibly) but soon the words became sharper, crisper, almost audible. I had no idea whether or not these people were my jailors or simply happened to live next door, and at the risk of incurring punishment I began to kick frantically against the wall, hoping to attract attention. Almost at once the woman's voice said, "He's kicking! He wants to be out of there!" So – the woman was part of the conspiracy. As I fell back into the darkness in despair I heard the man's loud laugh. In the days that followed, only too aware of the futility of my actions, I kicked at the wall out of sheer bad temper and spite.

In time I became aware of a third voice. It was a rather brisk, bland, paternalistic voice and it belonged to Dr Lopp. My jailors seemed to be worried about my condition. I was not surprised, I was beginning to worry myself. I had put on so much weight that I could barely move. My head and limbs were pressed tightly against the prison walls. Sometimes I wondered how I managed to breathe in such a cramped, confined space. There were moments of sheer blind panic as I wondered how I could possibly take much more. At such moments Dr Lopp's voice always seemed to intrude, with a banal "Nothing to worry about" or a "Perfectly natural in your condition". Whose condition? What about my condition? I had plenty to worry about. There I was, buried alive like someone in an Edgar Allan Poe story. There was no door in my cell. They would have to smash through a wall to get me out. I might die! I would be lucky to escape with severe bruising and lacerations to face and scalp!

Escape to what? I wondered afterwards. The wormshow? Theatrical, cruel and implausible events organised upon the curving surface of a large globe hurtling through space, vulnerable to collisions, explosions, innumerable disasters both natural and man-made, a world squeezed beneath capitalism and state capitalism, crawling with hungry worms beneath every foundation stone and bed of roses and green, well tended lawn. *El gusano amaestrado con possibilidades infinitas!*

After 46 weeks even Dr Lopp became a little anxious. After a year he decided the matter was best hushed up and dealt with in a private nursing home. I remember being transported here and there, poked and prodded, cruelly jolted, woken up without warning, and being generally treated without any consideration whatsoever. Once or twice I was even taken, bundled up in my sleeping bag, blind-folded, into a cinema where I was obliged to listen to the soundtrack of *Madness of the Heart* and *The Astonished Heart* and *The Small Back Room*. Probably, possibly, surely not, and yet perhaps as a result of this shocking experience it finally happened. Earth tremors occurred, initially mild, then severe. A massive force took hold of me, crushing me, squeezing me, forcing me towards a distant watery light. Huge spades of wood were jammed against the sides of my head and turned slowly, causing me excruciating pain. With a final massive explosion of blood and slime I was brought out into a bare, unattractive room smelling of raw meat and disinfectant, where a masked giant bore down upon me with a pair of scissors and a determined look in its eyes.

And that is the story of how I was conceived at sixteen minutes past eight on a sunny August morning in 1945 and remained in my mother's womb until my birth at one minute past midnight on April 1st 1950. When I look back over that strange, dark phase of my life, I can only assume that my mother's body, intoxicated by what it had learned, through osmosis, from her mind (she was a great fan of Trotsky and Victor Serge) was spontaneously attempting, out of kindly charity and in defiance of all biological orthodoxy, to delay for as long as possible my entry into that golden age of Labour government when, under that great leader MIST-AIR-HAT-LIE, food and clothing were rationed and workers had to get by on a weekly ration of thirteen ounces of meat, one-and-a-half ounces of cheese, six ounces of butter and margarine, one ounce of cooking fat, eight ounces of sugar, two pints of milk, and a solitary egg, when striking dockers, gas workers, miners and lorry drivers were denounced, spied upon and prosecuted, when, on eighteen different occasions, the government sent troops across picket lines to take over strikers' jobs, when, for the first time in British history, compulsory military service in peacetime was introduced, when conscripts were sent off to fight and die in Korea, when the goodwill of South Africa was actively sought and cultivated in exchange for gold and uranium, and when, in total secrecy, an atomic weapons programme was introduced.

I will shortly be fifty years old. I am almost completely bald and live in Croydon. I am an accountant. I have neither wife nor children. I wear glasses with anti-glare coated lenses, for safe vision with no irritating reflections. I adore watching old black and white films starring Kathleen Byron. I enjoy listening to Wagner and reading the works of Darwin. I vote Labour, always with the same deep misgivings. My life has been entirely lacking in excitement or incident apart from the time I attached a PAVEMENTS ARE FOR PEDESTRIANS sticker to the windscreen of a scarlet Ford Sierra illegally parked on the footway of Walker's Way, Penge, and my seven years as a Maoist guerrilla in Peru.

My earliest memory? My earliest memory is of lying sprawled upon my parents' lawn, tangled in the straps of my reins, wailing with fear and disgust at the slow approach of an earthworm, its dimensions hideously bloated by infantile perspective, extreme emotion and, later, by the awesome optical illusions created amid the muddy, backward surge of passing time.

General Jaruzelski's Sunglasses

Dark enticing pools of mystery ... Solid, dependable frames. A no-nonsense fusion of justice and authority. Balance.

1 – He has been sensitive to light since the age of twelve
He has been sensitive to light since the age of twelve. It was during the Great Patriotic War. A Panzer division was advancing in the usual ruthless fashion towards Wink. Horizons displayed pillars of black smoke and echoed with the conventional noise of field artillery – thunderous claps, the whizzing and whistling of projectiles. From the interior of a ruined cottage a wide-eyed grey-cheeked boy scrutinised the advancing column of grey armoured vehicles. A single thought throbbed in his small, partially developed brain. *Defend the Fatherland!* Catching sight of an abandoned mortar he ran forward and crouched beside it in the ditch where it conveniently lay. How his hands fumbled with the cold, complicated device. He paused and took a deep breath. He remembered the lesson given him two weeks earlier by Josef, a kindly old infantryman, now dead. Keenly his fingers went to work on the greasy knobs and levers. Slotting in a shell, the boy fired. *Whoompf!* As the road ahead erupted the Panzer Commander bared his teeth in the fashionable fury of the period. "Fire!" he screamed in German (with a slight Yorkshire accent). Almost at once puffs and whiffs and whoofs of smoke began to jig along the shattered walls of the cottage. Brief close-up of bullets penetrating an already shattered portrait of the Christ. A grenade exploded beside the ditch, scorching the boy's eyebrows and blinding him. He fell back, winded. Josef's kindly old face flashed in his mind. *Defend the Fatherland!* Josef had taught him how to load mortars in the dark, blindfolded and upside down. The boy reloaded the mortar. *Whoompf!* The Panzer Commander gave vent to the con-

ventional Nazi cries of fear and exasperation: _Gott in Himmel!
Da ist ja zum Kotzen!_ Surely there were a hundred or more of
the enemy lurking out there! The Commander feared an
ambush. Reluctantly he ordered a retreat. Hurrah! Wink was
saved.

The entire episode witnessed through X7 binoculars (powerful German ones once used in espionage work) by a far-off
friendly Soviet major. After the Germans had departed, the
Major made his way across the shattered smoking landscape to
the ditch where the boy lay. He found the lad in rags, still
beside the mortar, temporarily blinded, bravely groping in the
mud for unused ammunition. "Hello there!" cried the Major "I
am a friend from the Red Army, come to liberate the oppressed
Polish people." He reached down in comradely fashion to
assist the child. "Tell me your name!"

"Jaruzelski, sir. I am an orphan."

The Communist's merry eyes twinkled. "Well, my little man,
we must make a proper soldier of you, eh?" It was at that
instant he decided to adopt the boy.

And now the sunlight gushes across the face of the still-
blinded child. He begins to smile and solemnly nods his head.
A waxwing begins to sing amid the ruins. "Josef used to say,
sir, that a soldier's life is the best there is."

"Your friend Josef is a wise fellow."

"Was, sir. Was. He's dead now. He died for his Fatherland."

"Brave, good Josef. But come! We must find you a suitable
pair of sunglasses!"

2 – In the grey years

Forty-eight hours after the battle of Wink, his eyesight returned. But daylight was ever afterwards painful to Jaruzelski.
In the grey years of the nineteen-fifties and sixties the young
Jaruzelski led a charmed life. At the age of twenty-three he was
already in possession of fifty-six gleaming gold and silver
medals. His jackets sagged so much they needed constant
replacement. Despite his disability, Jaruzelski rose rapidly
through the ranks. The Major, who had remained in Poland

with many of his colleagues in order to offer fraternal assistance to its people, was delighted with his protégé's progress. "He will be a General one day, you mark my words."

His subordinates were in complete agreement. "He's a fine young man."

It seemed as if everyone who really mattered in Polish society had a friendly word for the handsome young officer with the sunglasses.

3 – Beautiful women

Beautiful women regarded the sunglasses as enigmatic and sexy. Jaruzelski wore them always – except in bed. Arguments about the true colour of his eyes inflamed the Polish people. Families were divided; wives left' their husbands. "They're blue, I tell you!" "Rubbish!" "Everyone in the Party knows they, are, in fact, dark brown." "Celeste says they are green – and she should know!" "Celeste's a lying whore!"

By 1962 the public demand for sunglasses had become so great that State warehouses were empty. Western tourists were stopped in the street and offered thousands of złotys. Some were dragged into medieval alleys and robbed. The authorities acted quickly. The famous June decree banned the wearing of sunglasses in public during the months of May, June, July and August. Exemption was granted only to those military personnel above the rank of Brigadier. In 1964 these exemptions ceased.

4 – His psychiatrist defected

Jaruzelski's psychiatrist defected. He hid in a container ship transporting eight tons of Theories of Surplus Value, Volume Three, from Gdynia to Wismar. There he stole a blue canoe and paddled by night to Eckenforde. Forged identity papers took him on to Hamburg and a ferry to England. Arriving at Harwich he slipped a note to Passport Control. The next day he found himself in a sparsely furnished room in a Sussex mansion. In the distance a crow was making a mechanical croaking sound. A middle-aged man of distinguished appearance motioned the psychiatrist to be seated. Over coffee and cognac the two men chatted amicably about the Second World War, the sights of Warsaw, the "Warsaw Concerto" and the tendency to decadence in the peoples of both east and west. Then, the small and medium talk over, they moved on to a discussion of General Jaruzelski's solitary vice. The General had a passion for liquorice. In particular, he craved Bassett's liquorice allsorts. The psychiatrist consulted an old notebook. He was able to reveal that Jaruzelski enjoyed allsorts both for their texture and their colour, which he found "bland", strangely "repressive", yet "soothing and comforting". The psychiatrist stated that the General often emptied a box of allsorts across his desk at military headquarters. Apparently he enjoyed stacking the sweets to make little coloured walls and castles. Of course these sugary constructions soon toppled over and then the General would fly into tremendous rages and punish the allsorts by imperiously sweeping them into his mouth and gulping them down. The interrogator nodded.

"Tell me," he said, slipping the question in casually, "why does the General wear those sunglasses?"

The psychiatrist shrugged. "Oh, those ..." he said wearily. "Everyone wants to know about those damned sunglasses. The fact is the General is crazy for American westerns. There is a song: 'Keep those wagons rolling, rolling, rolling, rolling'. You know? Bang! Bang!"

The interrogator shook his head. "But I still don't quite see ..."

The psychiatrist beamed. "Answer is easy," he replied. "Beep buddy-beep, buddy-beep, buddy-beep, buddy-beepedy-beepedy-beepedy-beep, dada-dumb, dada-dumb, dada-dumb-dumb-dumb!" He continued to beam. His cheeks were pink.

The interrogator sighed. How he loathed foreigners! Why was it always *him* who had to deal with Slavs? "I'm afraid I don't quite –" he began.

The psychiatrist grunted. Was the Englishman an idiot? "The General," he cried, crashing his vast fist upon the table top, "thinks he is – how you say? – your Lone Ranger."

5 – The periscope broke surface in a gunmetal dawn

The periscope broke surface in a gunmetal dawn. "The East Falklands, *mon general* – if I am not mistaken," said the Soviet submarine commander gruffly, squinting into the viewfinder.

"The East Falklands" echoed Jaruzelski, sighing enigmatically. But this is not the place to speak of his six weeks in the hills masquerading as a blind shepherd.

British journalists filed many remarkable stories concerning the strange properties possessed by those sunglasses. Helicopters navigated by them; fires were lit on windswept mountainsides; signals were flashed to ships on far horizons. Crucial short-wave messages were transmitted. On one occasion the General's sunglasses even succeeded in deflecting – but here I am governed by the Official Secrets Act and must fall silent.

One day a grateful nation will be told of that historic night-time meeting in a little room in Whitehall, when a stocky sunglassed figure in combat clothes was ushered into the presence of the two most powerful women in Britain. "Your Majesty, Prime Minister," said Jaruzelski, gallantly bowing, "It was nothing. *Pas du tout.*" Tears came into his courageous eyes. He spoke of Josef, of democracy, of the need for like-minded people to pull together in the face of the enemies of civilisation. He spoke of "a modest attempt to make a small repayment of the debts of 1939". The two women's heads nodded in unison. They were touched. They trembled. He was a handsome fellow and no mistake. Perhaps Communists weren't so bad after all – full of foolish wrong-headed ideas, but at heart holding simple and homely values, just as they did.

6 – An interview with General Jaruzelski

Arriving at military headquarters I was pleased to discover that the Polish People's Army is an equal-opportunity employer. Attractive young women could be seen at work in numerous offices, busily typing important state documents. Their stouter, maturer sisters were on their knees, scrubbing the worn linoleum until it gleamed like almost new. Even more enormous women pushed rattling trolleys bearing steaming urns of tea. I was led up to the sixth floor of the building and introduced to a leather-skinned man of a peculiarly dark complexion. Unlike the others in the building he did not wear jackboots or conventional military attire. On the contrary, his feet were enclosed in soft moccasins, and instead of a uniform he was dressed in a loin-cloth and a leather jerkin with tassels. Clearly he belonged to an elite special-action force. This remarkable individual muttered to me in guttural, incomprehensible Polish (with a slight Yorkshire accent) and signalled to me to follow him along the corridor. The walls of the corridor were green. We halted before an imposing panelled door. He knocked, a light above the door glowed red, and I was ushered in.

General Jaruzelski rose from an easy chair and took my hand. "You English," he said "are a remarkable people."

I felt the blood rush to my cheeks. "Yes," I replied, "I suppose we are."

I must be frank with you. I warmed to the General immediately. He seemed a kind, wise man. I found him surprisingly well informed about cultural developments in the west. He set me at ease at once, telling me how much he admired *Krapp's Last Tape*. He told me with a laugh that he absolutely adored John Huston's film *Wise Blood*. He confided shyly that after a hard day attending to the liquidation of anti-socialist elements he liked nothing better than to relax listening to the records of Ray Charles. With a sudden thrill of pride I noticed next to the portrait of Lenin a signed photograph ("All the best, Roy") of the great singer, Orbison.

General, why do you wear sunglasses?
The sunglasses were entrusted to me by the Parliament of the Polish People's Republic. I considered it my moral and political duty to accept an optical aid entrusted to me by the democratic representatives of our socialist community for the function of improved perception on the part of the head of state.

General, not only are you the first man in Polish history to unite the functions of Prime Minister, Minister of National Defence and First Secretary, but you are also the very first individual ever to occupy these positions while being, simultaneously, a dedicated wearer of sunglasses. Is this significant?

Only in so far as I am a member of the Polish United Workers' Party, the ideology of which is the signpost of my conduct, ensuring a healthy democratic relationship with workers in glassworks, plastics factories, the fields of engineering and chemicals, the disabled, and others for whom sunglasses form an important part of the Polish way of life and whose feelings on these and all other matters are expressed through a comprehensive system of civic consultative councils both at national and local levels.

But I don't quite see ...

Then perhaps you need sunglasses, my friend!

But if I could press you on this point, General. Some people would say that your sunglasses are of foreign manufacture, testifying to the stagnation and backwardness of the Polish economy under totalitarian military rule.

Who are these people? Their eyes require urgent medical attention. Believe me, my friend, here in the east we have some of the finest opticians in the world. Nowadays myopia and mydriasis are almost unknown in our country, not like in the bad old days.

But I can see the words from here, General, printed in small gold letters along the plastic arm: "Made in Hong Kong".

Filth! Liar! Keep your distance! Move away from me! Stay with the facts rather than your subjective interpretations. Be guided by sober analysis. One must see things in the correct perspective. I cannot permit my sunglasses to become a screen for destructive and chauvinistic forces hostile to the radiant flame of socialism. (Laughs.) But let us not quarrel. Let us be friends. Do you like allsorts? Let me call my man. Tonto! Tonto! Another packet this instant, do you hear me?

7 – It rained all day

It rained all day. All this was a long time ago. How quickly the world forgets! Grey clouds, grey buildings. Grey streets lined with sombre, silent troops. The barrels of their guns wept silent tears. In Wink a special mass was held. It was the day of Jaruzelski's interment. Half Poland seemed to have swarmed to the capital. Many of the spectators wore sunglasses, some out of respect, some to hide their tears, others because it made them feel good. Solemn party workers passed among the mourners distributing black liquorice drops. At eleven in the morning on that chill drizzling February day thirty-four bombers piloted by crack bomber pilots flew noisily overhead in formation. It seemed as if the sky itself was hiding its sorrow behind an immense pair of sunglasses.

$$
\begin{array}{ll}
\text{T T T T} & \text{T T T T} \\
\text{T T T T T T T T T} \\
\text{T T T T} & \text{T T T T}
\end{array}
$$

As the aerial droning faded, the gleaming coffin, pulled on a gun-carriage by six black horses, began its slow journey through the streets of Warsaw. Upon the coffin lid, folded now, next to the fifty-seven medals, unspeakably poignant, rested a pair of sunglasses, glistening and speckled with a host of silver drop-lets. A weeping Indian in sodden moccasins was seen to walk behind.

The Problem with the President's Mouth

A White House spokesman has denied there is any truth in the recent spate of rumours about the problem with the President's mouth. To quash idle speculation, and in a rare break with formality, the President's doctors have just issued the following press release:

His shape. The President remains ball-shaped. He is springy and flexible when he needs to be but tough-minded and bouncy if that is what the situation calls for. He is still the all-rounder he always was.

His wit. Sharp as ever. If, out of the blue, the President is asked, "How are you today, sir?" he at once replies, "Swell. And you?"

His teeth. Still white, still shiny. Polished, brushed and re-sprayed by specialists every morning at 11am on the dot, they need give no cause for alarm.

His warm smile. The President's warm smile is no ordinary warm smile. He does not mind folks knowing it is comprised of two thousand hand-sculpted nodules of high-grade polystyrene dyed pink by a top-class Manhattan artist named Henry Dorf.

His wind. Like most American males his age the President manufactures a goodly two cubic litres every twenty-four hours. A remarkable device worn under his golf windcheater permits 85% to be siphoned off by the military for use against foreign aggressors. The President wishes it to be known that he has strictly vetoed its use against women and children, even those with dirty complexions. The remaining 15% is dispersed in the night sky over Washington, with no risk at all to the public. In the past the presence of microphones attached to the President's windcheater has, admittedly, caused difficulties and even moments of embarrassment during abrupt and unexpected leakages. The President has said that he does not mind folks knowing that the problem has been solved by a high-tech-sulphur-detector-implant in his anal canal. When a rush of gas is detected approaching from the sigmoid colon an electrical malfunction is triggered in microphones and other television news equipment within a one-hundred metre range of the President. A simultaneous jamming mechanism causes ballpoint pens and hand-held tape-recorders to seize up. When the breaking of the President's wind is terminated (and on some days – he is an elderly man, remember – this may take up to twenty minutes) an invisible beam re-starts all the paralysed machines and the press conference proceeds as smoothly as ever.

It is an unspoken and generally accepted rule that no mention of such occurrences at press conferences be permitted. Jokes about this phenomenon and the President's liking for windcheaters are also strictly vetoed and any violation is likely to result in loss of credentials, loss of employment, and loss of status, followed by poverty, humiliation, degradation, squalor, and life termination by an employee or employees of the Central Intelligence Agency. However, the President has agreed to use of the following statement: *Sources close to the President confirm he has taken delivery of a Sulphur-Defence-Early-Warning System. The President is very proud that, with the exception of a handful of Japanese wires, circuits and microchips, the system is one-hundred-per-cent made in America.*

His mind. Average. Like 97% of all Americans, when faced with the written question, "What is an intellectual?" he ticks "A rare South American reptile" from the six possible boxes. If asked this question verbally, the President replies, "Could you spell that, please?"

His excreta. Never less than six inches in length and two inches in circumference. Light-brown in appearance, strikingly reminiscent of English-made Belgian-style milk chocolate containing a minimum of 20% of milk solids and a 25% minimum of cocoa solids. Inside are found small deposits of precious metals, curious pebbles which when washed are suitable for domestic display, pieces of bone both animal and human, as well as many intriguing fossil fragments which are a continuing source of fascination among those palaeontologists at our higher seats of learning who are privileged to be in receipt of them. Many important papers have been published and there is talk of an anthology. As for the knots of white, writhing thread-worm: they are, of course, extracted immediately, bottled, and distributed on a strictly egalitarian basis to high-schools up and down America, where they are a popular resource in human biology lessons and a ready source of instruction and interest among those many fine young men and women who are developing an interest in parasites.

The President's tears. Daily analysis continues to show beyond any doubt that they are one-hundred-per-cent essence-of-crocodile.

His hearing. The President's audiologist reports that after the President was played a thirty-minute tape of crying, malnourished babies in _____, the screams of torture victims in _____, the sobbing of women and the groans of bombed paupers in _____, the shrieks of _____ with severed limbs and the wailing of the dispossessed natives of _____, he chuckled and said: "Come on, Harry. Start the tape! I haven't got all day!" It cannot be emphasised too strongly that the President's hearing is one-hundred-per-cent.

His eyesight. The President's optician reports that when shown slides of the bodies of civilians around the world killed/mutilated/raped/tortured by _____ troops and the troops and state security forces of _____ supported regimes, the President commented: "That's one hell of a neat blank screen you got there, Al. When you gonna show me some pictures?"

His water. Passed at regular three-hour intervals, it has been much admired for the beauty of its transitions from a pale boiled-cabbage green to an evocative harvest gold which has caused even impartial observers to babble of sunset lakes in Vermont, the sands of Oregon, and late fall in the prairies. Holding up the frothy luminous flasks in order to examine them against windows and attractive lamps, laboratory assistants have been overheard by trained listeners. The assistants speak with excitement and enthusiasm of the richness, nuance and delicacy which emanate mysteriously from the President's unique and remarkable kidneys. Analogies have been drawn with the composition of string quartets and the writing of visionary poems. According to United Nations observers, the laboratory assistants have been seen pointing at the flasks' limpid, swirling contents and speaking in hushed, admiring voices of resemblances to the autumnal sky in Mon-et's *Varengeville Church,* of the wall above Mme Vuillard's head in Vuillard's *Madame Vuillard Sewing* and of the uneven grassy foreground in Seurat's *Le Crotoy, Looking Upstream.* Watching these young men and women as, white-coated, a little solemn, respectful of what they hold in their gloved hands, knuckles firm as they transfer the liquid into jugs and test-tubes, listening to them as they talk sombrely and soberly of luminous yellows and bravura diagonal brushstrokes, who for a moment could doubt that the rumours about the problem with the President's mouth are the work of Godless malcon-tents, troublemakers, Leninists even, who seek only to slur and subvert what is good and true and decent in this world? Who, gazing at the soft, muted contents of one of those glass jugs, could, even for a moment, doubt the President's soundness of mind and body?

Dear Blank

Dear _____,

Hello there! Another year has gone by and it's as if it was only last month we were taking down the Christmas décorations. Isn't it amazing how time flies! It seems like only yesterday that Jack and I were sitting down to decide which room to redecorate this year, and now it's December and we still haven't quite finished painting the bars in Julie's room! (Julie, incidentally, is now taller than ever. We agreed some time ago that before too long we would have to decapitate her. It was either that or raising the ceiling, which we just couldn't afford.)

In January we heard from Teddy in Papua. While swimming in Lake Oho he encountered a small plesiosaur, a creature previously thought extinct for millions if not billions of years. Teddy said it was a fascinating creature, but alas it bit off one of his testicles (I believe it was the left one, though Dave says not). However Teddy is still in the pink and as he wrote on his postcard, "You can get by with one of most things if you really have to!"

In a letter Teddy elaborated.

1. One *Weltanschauung*.
2. One cup, one saucer, one teaspoon.
3. One theory about the true identity of Shagspur, the writer.
4. One windmill.
5. One lung.
6. One chum.
7. One flipper.
8. One bureau-bookcase once owned by Wordsworth.
9. One old notebook containing the following sentences:
   (a) Please let me see that boiled butterfly, it may require butter.

(b) She made an expedition to the ironmonger's, where her mildewed mangle lay.

(c) The fish was quite right: my uncle ought to take it to a tanner.

(d) Ron sat in the mud: he was hot.

(e) She did not let the fat hag sit on the mat: she shot her with a Colt 17.

(f) The hen and the albatross were caught in Fred's flat; Fred is a filthy pervert and a Trotskyist.

(g) The duck had bad luck: it died.

(h) What a coincidence: Mike also dislikes pink lobes.

(i) Hot-tempered Jarrett hit the cyclist hard: the cyclist cried out in Cantonese.

(j) The cyclist had a crack in him: Dick ran to Dishforth for his Dostoyevsky.

(k) Tim did not like to smoke a pipe when the sofa was watching: he drank tea from a tin pot.

Remember Aunt Dot? In February we were saddened to receive a telephone call from the Home to say that Dot had passed on. However, by practising devil-worship and sacrificing a goat in the front room we managed to "make contact" as the saying is. Dot told us "the other side" was "like Miami", then her spirit evaporated with a hideous gargling noise like disappearing bathwater, leaving a disappointing odour.

Slim is fatter than ever. He sits in the park all day, picking his nose and listening to Linda Ronstadt records. He says that after he explodes he wishes his remains to be thrown into the Thames from the top of the Post Office Tower.

In March there was a moment of real sadness for us when a passing pterodactyl abducted Abdul. Remember Abdul? I am not at all sure I do, but the house seems strangely quiet without him. Our mutated bat, Nixon, has been rather grey of late, and I think I know why!

As if this wasn't enough, the dish ran off with the spoon. I never liked that dish. I never trusted it after what happened with the fork. I warned Jack but he just wouldn't listen. Men!

At Easter we rolled eggs on Parliament Hill Fields, one of which escaped into Camden and bounced along the gutter, generating a sequence of intriguing picaresque events:

1. A short-sighted Young Conservative tripped, fracturing his femur. "I want an explanation!" he cried.
2. An Hegelian lost his temper and punched a Latvian. "My brother caught his spade on a spike!" he shouted.
3. A trapeze artiste spilt her steroids. "It is because we like peaches!" she whispered.
4. Derek D. Ibdin fell through a crack in the earth's crust and plunged two-thousand metres into a lake of molten lava. "Please drop the latch!" he gurgled.
5. Plomer's wardrobe began to smell. "The hose-pipe will not cool the cow!" he laughed.
6. A layer of bourgeois intellectuals were [illegible].
7. The tempo of the development of the proletarian revolution in the West quickened. "Look at the book!" they shrieked.
8. Nicetas Choniates Acominatus's 21-volume *History of the Byzantine Empire 1180-1206* became an international bestseller. "My grandmother spent two days in a punt!" she sneered.

In May Jack went to a conference in Berlin and Julie and I changed the sand in her room, Dick went on a school outing to Switzerland, where his class helped local people to eat up disused funiculars.

You'll never guess what! Jack had his nose amputated in June. This was just before Barbara gave birth to the stoats. Frankly none of us was surprised when Geoff left her and ran off with the microwave.

The cats are all doing well, except for our beloved tortoiseshell, Flim-Flam. We warned Flim-Flam that if we ever found her reading *Lenin on False References to Marx and Engels* she would have to go. Sadly, on the anniversary of Kerensky's order for the arrest of Vladimir Ulyanov, we caught her with her paws on an open copy of *Lenin on War and Peace*. Flim-Flam's mewling squeal, "Tolstoy!", did not fool us for a moment. I snatched the booklet, shredded it between my lips, and fed it to Nixon. Sadly, we had to put Flim-Flam to sleep. We dropped her down the well. Then we threw a brick after her. Finally, just to make absolutely sure that our beloved Flim-Flam was truly at peace, we poured in our very last barrel of hydrochloric acid.

Our summer was once again spent in Bilge. This, of course, was when poor Christabel was swept out to sea and seized by the giant squid. In September we let Julie out for her annual walk around the yard.

The season of mists and mellow fruitfulness was a little unkind to us this year. Sorry to have to report that poor Harry was on his way to work when he was torn into many small pieces by a force at present unknown to science.

Dick said it reminded him of *Bedknobs and Broomsticks*.

No need to tell you what happened in November! In fact I'm not even sure if any of you are still alive! Dick died of radiation sickness a while back and Jack, of course, is horribly burned. We were grateful for small mercies, however, and the survival of our portable photocopier has proved a real boon.

Before he passed away Dick invented a new game. To play it all you need is a knife and six cockroaches.

Jack's smell has got much worse since the beginning of this month. Jill thinks we should [illegible] and eat him on toast.

In all, a lively and varied year. God bless.

PS. In the end we chose black for the bars.

A Quiet Morning for the Pound

It has been a quiet morning for the pound. You would never have believed the noise it was making last night. High-pitched inhuman squeals, wailings and an oblique grunting. The racket kept me awake for hours.

In this part of the city the noise seems louder than in other parts. Admittedly I live on a hill. Or perhaps it is the walls. In the library old postcards may be purchased. They show Edwardian labourers building the walls. No, Victorian. Stout and manly. Moustaches, aprons. Yet you can never be sure. The piles of bricks and the stacked beams look impressive enough. The moustaches align with other representations of the era. And yet, with a little effort and polystyrene ... When I tap the walls I hear odd, indecipherable noises. Not quite whisperings, not quite the slippage of sinister wires.

Hollowness everywhere.

I was up until three, humming Beethoven. At seven I woke, at eight I went out. In the market I observed worried faces. The potato-seller with the amputated thumb was not at all his usual self. The blonde fishwoman broke off from beating at the air with her raw pink fists.

"The pound," she said, her voice low, her face grim. So low, barely audible above the metallic whine of thronging wasps. "Last night. How the poor thing suffers so. Is there, by chance ..."

"Good news," I replied firmly. "I have come directly from my radio. A government agent has just read out the latest bulletin."

A passing pensioner must have overheard me, for without warning a starved, shabby-looking personage, bald and of indeterminate sex, clutched at my arm and rasped: "The pound – must know – for sweet Christ's sake have mercy on a poor sinner."

Before I could reply the creature collapsed on the cobbles, its face a ghastly white, close to the whiteness you often see in dead pensioners. Seven rivules of blood began to explore routes among the pebbles. The rivule threading its way slowly towards Mesopotamia attracted the interest of a family of rats which lived nearby under the hamburger stall. They sipped with excitement the new flavour.

With a kick, I sent the rats back to their mince and crouched beside the dying figure. I whispered what I had heard. The pensioner strained to catch my news, then closed its eyes. Its wrinkles re-formed in a reasonable approximation to a beatific expression. I was at once reminded (I cannot help myself, these cultural spasms come upon me without warning) of Michel-angelo's "Entombment".

My mind shivered pleasurably as the analogy entered and spread. An ambulance hee-hawed closer. A crowd gathered. "He knows!" shrieked fishwoman, gesturing in my direction, hysterical. "He heard it just now. On his radio!"

I raised my arms. "My friends," I said. "Do not over-excite yourselves. The pound has passed a quiet morning. There is no cause for alarm."

A spontaneous cheer broke from the throng. A handful of individualists began applauding in the style made popular by Chinese Communism. The phrase "a quiet morning" buzzed from person to person. The corpse, meanwhile, had attracted its quota of flies. This distracted attention from the wasps, which had been switched off and were now being packed away in their box, next to the deflated rats.

Two smiling ambulance men wrapped the body in a rug and slid it into their vehicle. The crowd dispersed. Sunlight poured from a gap in the clouds. Someone was whistling "The Blue Danube". Potato-man spat joyously in the gutter and began to scratch his stump with slow, satisfied motions.

Heading home with my cod, I was tracked by a black cat.

The postman ceased whistling "Telstar" and nodded at me as I rounded the corner.

"That's a fine corner."

"It certainly is," I might have answered, but instead I gave him the honest truth. "I have been rounding it for many years

131

yet it remains at an acutely painful angle and causes me considerable mental distress."

"Hmm. Done something to your hand, have you?"

"A little. But bear in mind that before the first flint could be fashioned into a knife by human hands, a period of time probably elapsed in comparison with which the historical period known to us appears triflingly insignificant. Most people, if asked to spell out the difference between ape and man, would probably refer to brains, the mind, consciousness. Yet it is surely in the hand that one sees the great gulf between the lack of development of even the most man-like apes and our kind. The human hand has been perfected by thousands of years of labour. The number and general arrangement of the bones and muscles are the same in the hands of both ape and man, yet the hand of the lowest savage can perform hundreds of operations that no simian hand can imitate. No simian hand has ever fashioned even the crudest stone knife, let alone posted a letter or – worse – delivered one."

The postman nodded. "Letterboxes!" he spat. "Some of 'em's like mousetraps. But the ones I really hates is them wot's got draught excluders across 'em. It's like trying to push *Tristram Shandy* into the mouth of a dog with lockjaw."

"But Charles, please. Why the exaggerated working-class accent? You are beginning to sound like Stanley Holloway in *Brief Encounter*. I know perfectly well you were born and brought up in Guildford, have a doctorate in the novels of Fontane and are a skilled performer on the lute. Not to mention your deep-seated belief (borrowed from a book, and why not?), which you enthusiastically articulate whenever we meet, that in recent years we have been witnessing the decay of the global economy rather than the evolution of a fund-amentally new and different system of production and exchange, a decay characterised by declining profit-rates, globally synchronised business cycles, volatile exchange-rates and internationally mobile money capital seeking speculative investments."

"Sorry. It's all those old black-and-white movies from the

golden age of British cinema I keep watching. And the uniform. And the attitude of the public. You're the only person on the round who's even heard of Lyotard, let alone perceived correctly that his appeal is to those former radicals of the Sixties whose political disillusionment has been paralleled by their rise to professional, managerial or administrative positions serving the interests of Western capitalism."

"True. But the point I was trying to make was that the hand is not only the organ of labour, it is also the product of labour. Labour, adaptation to ever new operations, the inheritance of muscles, ligaments, and, over longer periods of time, bones that had undergone special development and the ever-renewed employment of this inherited finesse in new, more and more complicated operations, have given the human hand the high degree of perfection required to conjure into being the pictures of a Raphael, the statues of a Thorwaldsen, the music of a Paganini or a short story by Ellis Sharp. (My particular favourite is "To the Wormshow".) But as the organ and product of labour has developed, so, too, have modes of production, culminating in the capitalism which prevails today."

"A sad, sad tale to be sure," said the postman, shaking his head. He swung his gaze to a passing cloud which bore an uncanny resemblance to Jane Austen. "Have you heard?" he went on, handing me a sinister brown envelope. "It has been a quiet morning for the pound."

"Yes," I said. "I heard the bulletin."

"Good. I'm pleased."

Silence suddenly impregnated the desolate street. A violin concerto began to crawl into my mind. Much to my surprise (for nothing at all like this had occurred in earlier drafts of "A Quiet Morning for the Pound"), Charles walked a few more paces then disintegrated into nine jagged sections, like a broken pot or plate.

This came as an enormous shock to Charles, too. Nothing like this had ever happened to him before (or would again). In previous versions Ellis Sharp had been content to leave him in the full flush of life, his pipes throbbing, his heart pumping vigorously, with half a lifetime of as-yet-unread classics, pints of beer, tots of whisky and thousands of rolls of unused soft lavatory tissue ahead of him on the golden horizons of his future. Now he was just a few shards of broken chinaware, with a rather banal pattern of daisies across what had previously been his chest. It was deeply upsetting for Charles to discover after many years that he'd all along been an inanimate object, cleverly fashioned to appear human but in fact nothing more than a cheap milk jug, utterly devoid of psychological depth or a rich, complex, rainbow-hued inner life of memory and desire.

We laid out the fragments of Charles in a clean shoebox and buried him at dawn in Highgate cemetery, not far from the original grave of Marx. Distant-flowered Sedge grows there, and Elongated Sedge and reddish Few-flowered Sedge, and sometimes the plume moth caterpillar feeds there, feasting on wormwood and *Teucrium,* oblivious to time and death and the erratic and unruly behaviour of sterling in the late capitalist era.

Goodbye, old jug. Goodbye.

Giacinta's Clams

La création du monde, c'est sérieux et mystérieux aussi. Histoires pour rire, langages bizarres et fautes d'orthographe, injures, monologues, pensées et proverbes, charades et problèmes à dormir debout, imitations et mensonges ... Il y a mille façons de jouer avec les mots.

Ellis Sharp, *Deux ou trois façons d'inventer le monde*

1

What is knowledge? What is a clam? Where is Giacinta today? Knowledge is a clear and certain perception of that which exists. A clam is a species of bivalve mollusc. The current whereabouts of Giacinta are unknown.

2

I will tell you everything I discovered about Giacinta. The rest is ash and dust. Knowledge is cognition, learning, erudition, information, acquaintance with any fact or person. Knowledge is cognizance. Knowledge comes between "Knottiness" ("the quality of being knotty"), "Knout" ("A whip with a long triangular thong used as an instrument of punishment in Russia") and "Knubs" ("waste silk produced in winding off from the cocoon, afterwards carded and spun"). After knowledge comes the silence of moths, the brittle heaps of dry discarded clam shells.

3

The moment I read about Celine, Giacinta and Clara I wanted to know more. My motive was naked curiosity, nothing else. I had no sober motives. I was not really interested in the light they might be able to shed on R-------r's character, or any nonsense of that sort. Celine, Giacinta and Clara were intriguing creatures in their own right. The rational thing to do was to start looking for Celine. Much more was known about her than about the other two. A rational person would have placed notices in the French and Italian press, spent at most three years trying to trace her, and then given up. As you will come to appreciate, I am not a rational person. There was less known about Giacinta than about either of the other two. You must also remember that at this time in our nation's history there were relatively few private investigators to turn to. Of the handful of agencies that existed only two boasted bilingual detectives and in both cases the second language was French. Giacinta, Giacinta. I think it was the teasing tantalising melody of those sensual and chewy vowels, the way they embraced and bit ravenously into the hard pulsating muscular consonants. Celine, by contrast, was a mere slurred hiss. Celine had no word appeal. I knew that if I ever met Celine she would turn out to be metallic, with a slight whirr. As for Clara. Clara was strangely redolent of jugs and churns, thick cream and red wholesome cheeks. Clara stood for health, and I wanted something different, something with a faint ambiguous perfumed reek of sickness and depravity, I had an intuition that if I ever touched Giacinta her skin would turn out in be thrillingly clammy. Two subsidiary factors favoured my choice. Giacinta had been number 2. Number 2 always finds out about number 1 and is invariably a bubbling boiling acid vat of information about number 3. Giacinta was Italian, and Celine was known to have left Paris and gone to live in Italy. Dobson agreed that Italy would be a good place to begin. It was dirty, with many blind alleys and steps, ideal territory for private detective work. It was quite unlike France, which was windy, with towers.

4

Like everyone else I first came across the story of Celine, Giacinta and Clara in 1848. At the time it never occurred to me to try and track any of them down. Times were hard. My nose itched. The harvests were bad. It rained a lot. Sea-serpent sightings were the lowest for seventeen years. Business underwent a slump. In January the people of Palermo ran riot in the streets. In London in February, a couple of foreign rabble-rousers published their *Manifest der Kommunistischen Partei.* It continued to rain a lot. In March every Frenchman over 21 was given the vote. On the first day of April I put on my gorilla costume and frightened the maids, one of whom foolishly broke her leg. In May there was unrest in Zug. On 12 June Radetzky captured Vicenza. In July Austria won a great victory at Custozza. There was talk of reinstating the Dhey of Algiers. It was quite the wrong time for someone of English nationality to be wandering around asking questions about strange women. In August Windischgratz crushed Prague. September saw Kossuth appealing to the Constituent Assembly of Vienna. There was no let-up in the rain, In October I caught a chill and took to my bed, where I read half a dozen of the season's new novels. In November Felix Schwarzenburg was made Prime Minister of Austria. By December my thoughts about Giacinta had to take second place to the dreary, wearisome obligations of Christmas. 1849 wasn't much better, what with the rain, the blockade of Venice, revolts in Baden, Bavaria and Saxony, and insubordination by the draymen of Barclay and Perkins breweries. In short, the quest for Giacinta did not begin until 1850, on the same rainy day in October that the single-volume edition of *The Personal History, Adventures, Experience, & Observations of David Copperfield, The Younger [Which He Never Meant to be Published on any Account]* first appeared.

5

The first impediment was the language difficulty. Canel spoke Hebridean Gaelic (Outer) which was better than nothing. Schulz had attended a performance of *Nabucco* which he pronounced "a most agreeable evening". Friedman was interested in gladiators. Only Walsh, a sly fat little man who collected matchbox labels, looked as if his heart might not be in it. The four men began a crash course at the Garibaldi Institute, an unimpressive one-room establishment run by a Genoan radical in a cul-de-sac in Soho, Seven months later, in April, they were fit for Italy. Canel devoted himself to the coastal region around the Golfo di Squillace. Friedman plunged into the stinking streets of Naples. Walsh said he'd begin with Turin and Milan. Schulz proposed to work his way methodically down the Adriatic coast until he met Canel. Dobson coordinated the hunt from his third-floor office in Regent Street. One wall was dominated by an enormous map of Italy. The map identified the major towns and highways and those areas more than thirty metres above sea-level, as well as public lavatories and important windmills. Over the next four years Dobson struck a very great number of pins into this map. The pins were coloured red, blue, green, pink, white, yellow, and mundane. Mundane was a colour Dobson himself had invented. It is best described as a sort of purply yellowish grey. After four years I think even Dobson had forgotten what the pins represented. In the meantime the Government had become interested in Dobson's new colour. It had been decided to paint all government buildings mundane, both inside and out. Dobson was startled to receive in the post one morning an order for 100,000 gallons of mundane paint (gloss). Fortunately for me, before Dobson had time to withdraw his agents from Italy *and* re-train them in paint manufacture, he was arrested. His cleaning woman, suspicious of his foreign map, had reported him to the police. Dobson was charged with engaging in unlawful military manoeuvres and conspiring to act in a suspicious manner likely to be of assistance to the enemy, under the Suspicious Foreign Maps Act, 1811. The jury returned after two minutes and pronounced Dobson guilty. He was sentenced to thirty-five years. On his way to Wormwood Scrubs Dobson overpowered his guards and fled to Hyde Park. There he stole a hot-air-balloon and drifted, initially at a height of five-hundred feet, towards the City of London. In those days the White Tower had a golden weather vane attached to its roof. The weather vane was in the shape of a cockerel. The cockerel had a beak, His balloon hit the beak at a velocity of forty-seven miles-per-hour.The explosion was heard as far away as the Garibaldi Institute in Soho. Dobson's house and office were ransacked but no formula was ever found, and the secret of mundane died with him.

6

Quite what Canel was doing in Venice I have never been able to fathom. The circumstances of his death there are sketchy. Apparently he was seen feeding some pigeons by a holidaying Texan. The Texan distinctly remembered a nearby church pealing two. Canel was wearing a yellow kilt and balancing a bucket on his head. He was throwing rashers of raw bacon around. Pillars of ecstatic pigeons shimmered in the sweltering air. Five minutes later my detective was observed in the canal, shouting something at a party of pupils from the Convent of the Sacred Mother School for the Deaf. Naturally they assumed Canel was something to do with the carnival. "In Italy," wrote Friedman, "it is the custom for local people to gather in the streets in order to watch a burlesque wooden-frame figure made from straw and purple crepe be dragged past. Bullets are fired into the figure, and casualties are many. Last year alone fifteen women, forty-two men, three dogs, and a blind donkey were fatally injured in this way. When dusk falls the burlesque figure is ignited, often resulting in severe burns to spectators in the first five rows. Whether or not these facts are of relevance to the death of Canel can, at this stage, only be a matter of conjecture." Canel's skill at holding his breath under water for over one hour impressed and delighted his audience. The carabinieri were not called for another two hours. They decided to leave the body where it was until after the fireworks, so as not to put a damper on things. A stray firework set light to the roof of the Venice opera house, and as you will certainly remember, many streets were destroyed and three canals evaporated in the heat. This further hindered the recovery of Canel's remains.

Fortunately for his next of kin, the bucket, clearly marked "Made in Birmingham", greatly assisted in the identification of the corpse. Schulz was able to reveal to the coroner that Canel had been homesick for Edgbaston since day one of his arrival in Italy. The bucket had been his mother's. An examination of Canel's brogues revealed microscopic traces of bacon on the soles. Schulz, who had for many years believed that pigeons were alien creatures being manipulated by an advanced civilisation on Saturn, suggested that a pigeon had deliberately dropped a rasher in front of Canel as he stood on the bank watching the sun go down, causing him to slip and fall in. The coroner, however, decided that Canel was unbalanced, which, as Schulz pointed out, was a contusion almost identical to his own.

7

Bland replaced Canel. I did not warm to him. He was somehow greasy. I have never liked moustaches. If I had not been busy coordinating the search for Giacinta I am almost certain I would have initiated a statistical investigation into the links between criminality and facial hair. Bland, who was fluent in Italian, went straight to the Basilicata region. There he crossed the mountains, living on goat's milk and fried eggs. Another two years went by. A third. One morning I received a communication from Friedman and Schulz. It was a joint letter of resignation. They were, they said, sick of the name Giacinta. Between them they had interviewed 227 Giacintas, none of whom was the one I was after. They felt that farther search was futile. For all anyone knew Giacinta was living in South America, it was like looking For a – But here rain had seeped into the envelope and smeared the ink. My magnifying glass did not help me to identify the four missing words. The disfigured section of sentence seemed to rend "like looking for a noddle in a hiccup" but this, I knew, could not be right. I realised at once that since the missing words merely formed part of a simile they were not, in themselves, of any intrinsic significance. They were there to illustrate a point and the point was that they regarded the hunt for Giacinta as impossible. Unimportant? Yes. But I abhor a mystery. I was maddened beyond endurance by those blurred words. "Like looking for a nibble in a hockpack?" No matter how I played with the letters I could put no shape or sense at all into that ghostly outline of mutilated language. For twelve weeks I constructed long columns of letters and set to work exploring all the possibilities. I calculated that there were, in all, 877,244 permutations involved. During this period I did not go to bed until 3am at the earliest, and I was up again at dawn, poring over my calculations. It was my good fortune to crack the code on the eighty-fourth day, at the 319,118th attempt. The quest for Giacinta, Friedman and Schulz had written, was "like looking for a noodle in a pasta". Of course! I was a fool not to have spotted this before. I poured myself a large brandy to celebrate. As I raised it to my lips there came a knock at the door. It was my butler, bringing a postcard from Walsh.

8

My butler was a bald man in his early forties. He wore black outer clothes, white underneath. His unreal name was Brian, the uninventive choice of his parents, John and Jane, a dismal and lamentable pair. They hailed from Hayling, a dismal and lamentable isle. My butler's father had once found a coin from the reign of Charles I on the beach, but otherwise his life had been uneventful. They ran a boarding house, popular with clergymen and their wives. Cropper (as I decided to call Brian) was everything a butler should be. He knew how to prepare a cup of coffee. He appreciated how loathsome cold or lukewarm toast is. He was a bully and a royalist. He admired and respected wealth. He made sure that the other servants were servile, with the exception of Pierce. Pierce was my one-armed gardener, and the garden was outside Cropper's domain. Not everyone would have wanted a one-armed gardener, but Pierce was muscular and strange. He dead-headed roses with dexterity, split fallen trunks with his cleaver and a broad smile. Pierce, unlike my previous gardeners, had an encyclopaedic knowledge of crustaceans. Cropper, by way of contrast, had two arms and no tattoos. Cropper, like all the best servants, was an invertebrate. He was pleasingly deferential. Whenever I expressed an opinion he cocked his head to one side as if considering my point of view, and then nodded in a gratifying way, as if I was absolutely correct and there was nothing else of value to be said on the subject (which, in point of fact, there never was). Most of all, Cropper gave no sign whatever of possessing an inner life. This lack is the most valuable negative asset a servant can have. Pierce, unfortunately, had an inner life, but I was prepared to overlook this since he was never permitted to enter the house. Pierce lived in a sort of home-made shack which vaguely resembled a beach hut. He had painted the walls with pink and white stripes. The pink stripes were 800mm wide, the white ones 900mm wide. The domestic servants lived in the loft, or in the coldest rooms, especially those afflicted by damp and mould. Whenever I employ someone, especially if it is a woman, I always ask them if they have read *Jane Eyre*. Those who say that they simply adore the Brontës, or who nod vigorously with brimming eyes, are removed from the house at once, and the dogs are set upon them. Although I am a broad-minded employer I absolutely forbid novels in the house. I have made a special point of providing every servant with an individual set of spillikins. Spillikins sharpen the mind, and encourage dexterity of the fingers. Cropper is now on his twenty-fifth packet.

9

"Returning London 21st May. Meet me Victoria Station platform 3. Noon. Walsh." I felt my pulse begin to race. Had Walsh found Giacinta? I knew him to be a steady hard-working person. He ate spaghetti sparingly and never consumed alcohol, except on Tuesdays, when he became blind drunk. Walsh began each day with ninety-nine press-ups, except on Wednesdays. I rarely saw him blink. Was he perhaps (my pulse slackened) bored? Was he going to leave me to my own devices and walk away from it all? Eight years, and still no trace of Giacinta, let alone the other two. I was not sure my devices would see me through to the end of the year. I was almost fifty. In the mornings grey hairs clung to my pillow like survivors from a sunken liner. My devices were growing rusty and had not been serviced for over three years. The harness which I used to wear in bed, strapped to my shoulders and supporting an iron corset which cleverly held a book in two steel claws, turning the pages by means of a jewelled crane powered by an impressive assembly of tiny cogs and movement of the triceps muscle (the muscle which, as every dwarf knows, is to be found within the olecranon of the ulna, to the rear of the elbow joint), thereby allowing me free use of both hands, a wonderful boon when reading, say, de Sade, was scandalously dusty. Dust, too, choked the mouth of my three-inch high mechanical Sir Thomas Browne. If I was to wind him, I wondered, would he still bend over his little book and part his painted metal lips with a rosy smile? Would Shakespeare, shapeless behind his ghost's sheet, still raise his little squeaky arms and grimace? Would Wordsworth sink to his knees and squat, in a defecator's posture, by that poignant clump of electroplated daffodils? And would De Quincey (the set was, alas, incomplete) raise a teaspoon to his lips in the old, whirring way and down his laudanum with a knowing wink? I had not the heart to wind up the machinery and try.

10

Walsh came panting up to the ticket-collector at three minutes past one. He was sweaty and apologetic. The train had been delayed (a suicide in Kent). There was no time to lose. We had to get to Dover as quickly as possible. We reserved all the seats in a first class carriage, and Walsh began to explain. He shook his head. No. Giacinta had not been found. He had returned because of Bland. Bland's activities threatened to discredit the quest. Bland's nose was gone. He had contracted a particularly virulent strain of syphilis and the disease had begun to rot his face. I am a broad-minded man, but Walsh had a point. A private detective without a nose is bound to attract attention to himself – especially when all there is in its place is a dark, sticky, stinking hole with guzzling flies perched on the glistening crusted rim. There was no other alternative: Bland must be fired. I gazed out of the window as Walsh described his plan. We were passing through a quaint little station with carefully tended wallflowers in pots and men scattering sand around the other track. By the time we reached the white cliffs the town was in darkness. Somehow we managed to get the cannon to the edge of the highest cliff. Together, we pressed Bland into the barrel. He raised no objection, having been coshed with the wooden handle of a knout some minutes earlier. As I pushed at Bland's head I kept my eyes shut, not wanting to catch a glimpse of his face. Walsh aimed at the dog-star and fired. The echo of the explosion broke a window in a greenhouse six miles to the north. The largest section of the breaking glass left a shape which exactly matched the configurations of Zanzibar. At the time we did not know it was low tide. The body was never identified. Bland's replacement, Hocke, proved a disappointment. His skin resembled enamel. The word which summed him up was shiny. He had a marine air, and large, soft, friendly eyes. I had not foreseen that he would be decapitated by a dredger off Felixstowe. In preliminary tests (I was determined not to employ another syphilitic monolinguist) both Walsh and myself repeatedly warned Hocke not to go swimming at night disguised as a seal. Hocke would not listen. I was astonished to read in his obituary that he had been deaf since birth. Walsh shrugged and scratched his left cheek. He returned to Italy alone on the last day of October. Eleven years had passed – and still no trace of Giacinta. On 2nd November Walsh found her, by accident, as I had always known he would.

"Celine!" said Giacinta with a soft low laugh. "I remember her well. What can I say? She was a woman. She had a woman's body. Ten toes, two thumbs, a head-shaped head. She was much as women are." Walsh had imagined the moment he would first set eyes on Giacinta on many occasions, especially Tuesdays. The words she would say to him were written in his head, and when she did not say them it came as something of a surprise. "Celine?" said Giacinta, perplexed. And then: "Oh, her. Yes, I knew her." Silence. "What more can I say? I liked her. She laughed a lot. She had a sense of fun. She used to dye dumplings orange and leave them steaming on park benches. I have seen her swing through the trees, agile as an orang-utang, reciting Milton. At first Edward was charmed by her gaiety. He tried to join in, cutting lozenge-shaped holes in his shirt and inserting carnations. Day after day he hacked at his shirts, until it wasn't funny anymore. His chest was covered in scratches and the apartment he had rented for her was covered in knubs and fragments of silk and cotton. In the fourth week of their relationship Edward audibly broke wind. Celine pretended not to hear. She spent most of his money on perfumes and incense. The drains of the Fourteenth Arrondissement and Edward's exhalations were a considerable trial to a young girl like her. Edward did not understand. He ate too much celery. Celery is 95% air and water, but Edward was a risk-taker. Soon he acquired the knack of breaking wind every hour, on the hour. Celine did her best to regard this as an engaging trait, idiosyncratically English, but her heart was not in it. Edward became addicted to beetroot. Each morning he ate a 7lb beet for his breakfast. It was bad for his complexion. It was only a matter of time before his explosions became twice-hourly. He became terrified of fire and absolutely forbade smoking, open fires, or the use of candles. Soon, by regular practice and deft muscular movements he was able to master this twice-hourly explosive roar and squeal. He created a dazzling pattern of tonic-subdominant-dominant-tonic harmonies. Holding a hand-kerchief to her nose, Celine staggered out into the night. The handkerchief had been made in India and was embroidered with elaborately stitched bullocks and drums. She ran to her brother's house. Pierre, an actor, famous for his Iago, agreed at once to wear his trumpet-major's costume. Celine knew that Edward would be skulking behind a curtain, trembling with jealousy. Pierre clattered his stage boots and made a pretty speech, full of jokes about Englishmen. Celine alluded to Edward's horror of cigars. She made a joke about his webbed feet. Edward hurled back the curtain and stormed into the room, quivering and querulous. "Is only a jock!" screamed Celine, but Edward took no notice. He kicked Pierre in the crotch, smacked a fist into Celine's face and ran out into the night, tears boiling down his cheeks. Two weeks later, in Bologna, he lay in my arms, whispering of clams."

12

"In the village of Drumconrath in Ireland," Walsh scrawled on the back of a postcard with a blurred picture of a gondola, "there used to be some old women who, having ascertained from Scripture that the hairs of their head were all numbered by the Almighty, expected to have to account for them at the day of judgement. In order to be able to do so they stuffed the severed hair away in the thatch of their cottages. But in the Upper Vosges they say that you should never leave the clippings of your hair and nails lying about, but burn them to hinder sorcerers from using them against you. For the same reason Italian women either burn their loose hairs or throw them into a place where no one is likely to look for them. I am as yet insufficiently intimate with Giacinta to ascertain her own beliefs in this matter, but rest assured I will leave no stone unturned. Sincere best wishes, Walsh."

It was in 1845, while on holiday with my daughter, that I first became something of an expert on burrida. The best burrida in my opinion is made from the uranoscopus scaber or star-gazer fish. Cut away the spiky bits, give the large intestine a playful squeeze, rinse the fish in vinegar and then toss it into a clay pot filled with mashed tomatoes, two tablespoons of olive oil, a cup of water, a bowl of mushrooms and a few slices of conger eel. Watch that the pot doesn't crack while the stew is cooking. If it does you may require treatment for severe burns, so do make sure you have the address of the nearest physician before you start hacking away at those difficult bits. Simmer for a good thirty-five minutes, or an evil three-quarters of an hour. At this point you can add just about anything you want to – breadcrumbs, sour cream, mildewed grapes, the choice is yours. But don't, whatever you do, forget to add the clams. I must admit, as I look back on those smoky little Genoese restaurants where my daughter and I gorged ourselves on burrida and delicious freshly baked bread, I little thought how the humble clams we swallowed would one day link us irrevocably with Miss Brontë's abominable book. Far from it. At the time we were much more interested in the exciting new ideas of Charles Fourier, in particular his brilliant suggestion that road repairs, the killing of vermin, and slaughterhouse work should be the monopoly of organised groups of small children. Small children, Fourier reasoned, adore getting dirty, and in response to carping objections that their height was inadequate for certain tasks, he pointed out that stilts are easily mastered, and that those children who had had their legs crushed by industrial machinery should not be allowed to use this as an excuse to shirk – not in a nation with perfectly adequate supplies of Shetland ponies.

14

Was Giacinta unprincipled and violent? Walsh said she gave

no sign of it. On the contrary, she reminded Walsh of cushions. He had made arrangements for his matchbox collection to be stored in the vaults of a bank in Geneva and was now writing a monograph on cushions in his spare time. "Cushions," he wrote, "are too easily taken for granted. They are of benefit to midgets faced with tables; they are a friend to the dying ... " He learned that her father had choked to death on a pastry, but made no mention of the filling. I felt that Walsh was no longer the Walsh I had known in the old days. He was losing his grip. Walsh, the old pro, was disintegrating. Were Giacinta's clams more interesting than her claims? She ran a fish restaurant in Oppogia, in Machiavelli Square. She had an enormous fund of stories about bivalve molluscs and crustaceans in general. For example:

(i) the story about the clam and the castrato;
(ii) the story about the shirt and jacket arms she had found inside the stomach of a large crab;
(iii) the story of the mussels, the dancer, and the diseased General.

Walsh had dropped in for breakfast (the bridge overhead had some planks missing, and Walsh had lost his spectacles only the day before). As he stood in the semi-darkness, stunned, blinking, circular tables materialising in the gloom, he heard someone in the kitchen shout "Giacinta!" A tall, handsome woman in her mid-thirties emerged from behind a wooden mermaid, crossed the restaurant and went into the kitchen. Walsh felt his heart begin to throb. "Raw or cooked, signor?" Raw, with pepper and a slice of lemon. Outside it began to rain.

15

She claimed that R------- (or "Eedurvard'‚' as she called him) was amusing, morose, childish, sensitive, brutal, sincere, stout, brilliant, devious and difficult to understand. "He said I was like my clams – voluptuous, pink and peppery.' His appetites were broad. Their relationship lasted six months ("Not three!" she cried in surprise). "And Clara?" "The daughter of a lepidopterist. Her father adored Zuppe di Pesce. They were touring the ruins, looking for moths. In Oppogia is many, many moths. Her father had to return to Berlin unexpectedly. It was the start of the rainy season. She and Eedurvard play many, many game of chess together at that table number over there, number 23. I think he was bored of my clams and curves." He wanted something cheesy and straight. Clara was a creature constructed out of twigs. She smelled of Gorgonzola. Her breasts were fantastic rumours. "I knew eat was over, so I hit him with a wet conger and sent him packing. When he finish his packing he and Clara go away to the mountains. She come back, weeping, the next summer. She sit at table 23 and tell me everything." Then she returned to Munich, only to be crushed by an elephant. Their affair had lasted a fortnight. Edward was restless and morose. His penis itched. He bought her a factory which manufactured artificial limbs. He told Clara a general European war was inevitable and that soon she would be rich. He was wrong. Now all she had was her memories and a warehouse filled with 4,000 wooden legs.

16

I sent Walsh a list of two hundred specific questions I wished him to put to Giacinta. Back came a postcard of the Spanish Steps and the message, "No use – she has clammed up completely." I despatched Walsh an angry telegram. A week passed, and then a fortnight. And then, one morning, Cropper entered with a package from Italy. Inside were eight fresh clams and a note from Walsh. "Giacinta and I were married on Tuesday. We are leaving Italy. Do not try and find us. There is nothing more to be said. Walsh." There was a postscript. "PS. Remember what I told you about Italian women and their hair? It's complete balls."

17

I opened the safe and took out my copy of *Jane Eyre*. I turned again, to the paragraph in Chapter XXVII in which Edward Rochester tells Jane about the women in his past: "I could not live alone, so I tried the companionship of mistresses. The first I chose was Celine Varens – another of those steps which make a man spurn himself when he recalls them. You already know what she was, and how my liaison with her was terminated. She had two successors: an Italian, Giacinta, and a German, Clara, both considered singularly handsome. What was their beauty to me in a few weeks? Giacinta was unprincipled and violent: I tired of her in three months. Clara was honest and quiet; but heavy, mindless, unimpressible; not one whit to my taste. I was glad to give her a sufficient sum to set her up in a good line of business, and so get decently rid of her."

I closed the book, inadvertently squashing a pair of moths between pages 310 and 311. It was all over for them, and all over for me. In the mirror I caught sight of a Mona Lisa smile on a rough, male face. It was a few seconds before I realised I was gazing at myself. It was then I realised the secret behind that enigmatic painted smile.

18

The moths had come a long way to these closely printed pages, and their screams must have been so low and squeaky that even their fluttery friends, had they been present (which they were not), could barely have heard or grasped the brief squashy anguish of their obliteration. The moths did not know that their fame was already behind them, back on the last page of Charlotte's sister Emily's book, where the dark fields of the West Riding roll on below the heights that whistle and whoop and wuther. Young Emily, a morose bad-tempered woman with a mouthful of rotten teeth, used often sullenly to prowl the moors. The two moths I had unintentionally wiped out had, in fact, been part of a merry crowd of nineteen moths spotted by Emily in Haworth churchyard on April 21st 1846 which she subsequently incorporated in the last sentence of the last page of her novel ("I lingered round them, under that benign sky: watched the moths fluttering among the heath and harebells ..."). Of these nineteen moths seven had been captured in Keighley by small boys and tortured to death, ten had emigrated to Finland, and the other two, after many picaresque adventures, had flown south and taken refuge in my wardrobe. A poignant irony, to be born in *Wuthering Heights* only to die inside *Jane Eyre*! Although tens of thousands of words have subsequently been written about the Misses Brontë and their books, I find it strange that no one has ever been interested in the identity of these moths. Unfortunately the spattered remains were of little use, bearing in mind the primitive state of the forensic arts at that time. There was little for me to go on, apart from the description in *Wuthering Heights* and the brown custard-textured sludge which smeared my *Jane Eyre*. I was tempted to say they were Coronet moths (Craniophora ligustri) which are commonly found in the temperate zone of the entire Palearctic (including Bradford), and which, like the families in Emily Brontë's novel, produce two generations. What almost clinched it for me was the discovery that Coronet moths in areas polluted by industry have a tendency to melanism, resulting in significantly darker forms. It was almost as if these moths were Heathcliff, Brontë's dark angel. But the claims of the Parsnip Moth, common in the vicinity of Haworth, were equally strong, as were those of the punningly appropriate Ericocrania haworthi or primitive moth. In the end, and after poking around in the splattery entrails of the corpses with a pin, I decided that what I had before me were unquestionably two dead White-points, one of the commonest moths of Europe.

19

The Mona Lisa smiles because she is pregnant! Inside her something is being brought to birth. And I, too, had brought something to birth. I had given birth to knowledge. In a strange, incomprehensible world (the ideas of Fourier have not caught on) I had redeemed Giacinta from the obscurity in which she would otherwise have rotted. Through Walsh, I had even given her love, and a new life. I never felt the need of a symphony orchestra more than at that moment, but instead of music a gust of ashes and dust swept through the room. It was Pierce, having one of his fires. He is a dull and stupid person but a good gardener. Pierce, seeing me at the window, waved his one good arm. His tattoo glowed in the sun. It portrayed a woman, naked apart from a scarf wrapped around her waist, sitting astride the blade of a gigantic knife, waving one arm and smiling. The knife pointed upwards at an angle of forty degrees, and around the handle cavorted two unicorns, a ruff and a mute swan. The tattooist had brilliantly executed the swan, even down to the ebony knob at the base of the upper mandible. Pierce's other arm had been eaten by a giant crab of an entirely unknown species, on the beach at Penzance, in July 1843. Pierce had lain down on the sand in a drunken stupor and had woken two-hours later just in time to see the monster scuttling into the waves, still chewing on its meaty prize. His jacket and shirt were both ruined. Afterwards Pierce visited libraries and consulted every English-language book about crustaceans that he could find, but in none of them was there any reference to a crab that remotely resembled the one that had eaten his arm. He returned to Penzance and took measurements. He made sketches and had them worked up into impressive illustrations by professionals. These, together with his jacket and shirt, he presented to the British Museum of Natural History. The zoologists there laughed at him and handed him back his mementoes. Pierce turned instead to the *Penzance Weekly Advertiser*. Soon he was something of a local celebrity. He gave talks on the pier. A "monster crab invest-igation bureau" was set up, attracting volunteers from all over the country. They lay on the shingle at dawn disguised as deckchairs. The great crab hunt lasted for two summers and then fizzled out. The audience for Pierce's pier talk dwindled.

He decided to go away and become a gardener instead. Pierce adored burning garden rubbish and hacking at things. He once told me that the enticing knottiness of the trees and shrubs in my twelve-acre estate were what made him apply for the job. He sliced chestnut with glee, scalding the lengths to kill off any fly. He bound them with wyth, stacking them in tens. His heart thumped each time he lit heaped twigs. Behind Pierce a rabbit ran across the lawn and disappeared in the rear of the monkey-puzzle tree. "Something must be done about that white rabbit," I reflected. I opened the top drawer of my desk and took out a sharp knife. "Pierce," I said, absentmindedly, lunging playfully at an imaginary flying crab while simultaneously brushing ash from my trousers. Cropper edged nervously away from me. A spillikin fell from his pocket and snapped underfoot. I remember I was in a good mood that morning. "Have a clam," I said, but Cropper shook his head, scooped up the splinters and ran from the room. I took a firmer grip on the knife and began slowly, skilfully, methodically, to prise out the succulent pink flesh.

The Aleppo Button

Life is full of horrors and hormones and so few things are
   certain,
So many unknown ...

Kenneth Koch, "The Art of Love"

With Hyerogliphicks quite dismembred,
And broken letters scarce remembred.

Henry Vaughan, "Vanity of Spirit"

1

So touched ... So touched by your presence. That you are able
to be here, more or less intact, wishing to learn what I have to
say about the Aleppo Button. In this foul weather, too. My
apologies for the change of venue, it seems there was a double-
booking. The pug show began yesterday and is a three-day
event, so I'm afraid shifting the kennels was out of the
question. This cramped lecture theatre in Biological Sciences is
all that was left. I apologise for the stench of wet fur and pug
droppings, not to mention the fug of ether, glue and
formaldehyde. I hope no one will be distracted by those shelves
of large, reeking glass jars containing the pickled remains of
small skinned animals or that embalmed human foetus
displayed at the back. So far so good. Before I continue let me
make one thing clear. I am not here to talk about the liturgical
preferences of the royal family, the stopping points of
peripatetic woad vendors in a previous era or Thayer's belief
that the earth and all other planets are constantly growing by a
method which involves sudden changes from the spherical to
the cubical form and back again. I am here to tell you about
one thing and one thing only, namely: the Aleppo Button.
Some of you may have inadvertently wandered in expecting to
hear a biology lecture, a solution to the riddle of why swans

sing before death perhaps, or why bees, which lack ears, are moved by music, or in hope of learning the reason why cacodaemons are put to flight by melody. If so, please leave, or if you wish, stay. Lastly, to ensure no misunderstandings, let me point out that Aleppo Button is not – repeat not – a celestial globe with hoops representing the different astronomical circles at the equator, ecliptic, etc., in their natural order and relative positions. It is not a term applied to the Grecian marbles collected by the Earl of Arundel and in the possession of the University of Oxford. Neither is it that which abounds with weeds. Nor is the Aleppo Button of the genus of bivalves in which the shell consists of a tube resembling the spout of a watering-pot of which the larger end is closed by a perforated plate. It is not a nuclear detonator trigger. It is neither a contraction of parts by application nor the stopping of constipation, still less is it a binding of a tenant of lands under Scottish law to grind at a particular mill. So far so good. I hope I make myself clear. Permit me to assert confidently (buoyantly, even) that the Aleppo Button has nowt in common with an Aleppo butt-end. Before I continue – incidentally, don't you find that foetus strangely reminiscent of Munch's *Scream*? – I have been asked to say a few words about myself. In view of the time, I will be brief. I was born in Poverty, a nondescript, windy little town in the north. Like other towns in the region it is famous for its sooty, banal, oppressive architecture and its numerous stunted giraffes. Later, as often happens to lusty young men, I met a woman. Rita, my Rita. Ah, love is a sand-fly crouched to prick amid the desert wastes of ordinary days! I had never met anyone as bonny and brilliant and buttony as her. Her lips were red, her looks were free. Her hair was long, her foot was light. Her carrot – My fingers flexed excitedly. I buttonholed her one morning, which she seemed to like. We drank coffee, we drank wine. We talked of *Toller,* of *Die Sorge des Hausvaters,* of *Die Verfolgung und Ermordung Jean Paul Marats dargestellt durch die Schauspielgruppe des Hospizes zu Charenton unter Anleitung des Herm de Sade*. I gnawed her lobes and kissed her ellipses,

I took off her chinchilla toque, I – Forgive me. I had too much to dream last night. Suffice to say we headed south to live in Sin, the popular resort. There, under the bright moon, we walked hand-in-hand by the disused funicular, listening to the wind sighing in the wires and watching the rust flake. Palm fronds clashed with their wild dry bitter sound against the bright glitter of the water, and a deep-blue second-hand haze spread like a carpet. We blushed and paled. *Iocus, & lusus!* Oblivious to our digestive functions, we embraced. We sank amid feathery ferns, chuckling at inquisitive passing fritillaries and a lone looper-moth. Passionately we transformed a mixture of oxygen, nitrogen and one or two other gases into carbon dioxide and water vapour. She was extraordinarily nimble. Her laughter was like the rustling of fallen leaves. She looked at me as she did love and made sweet moan. Side by side we lay in darkness, listening to the shipping forecast. We walked to the waterfall, the waterfall, the waterfall, which continues to churn and foam in my mind, its creamy detergent cleansing it of the long sequence of dislocations and adjustments that followed. In time we came to the inevitable Terminal. We talked of Trakl. Then, with tristful visage, I handed her a bunch of semantic iridescence. She rose slowly into the sky in a sealed tube and vanished in the direction of the stars. I shrank back with a hissing intake of breath to think of her drifting into that strange no-man's land where to follow people is impossible. The French have a phrase for it. The bastards have a phrase for everything and they are always right. I gawped stupidly at the white scar left behind her. Perplexed in the extreme, I trembled at her inflammatory absence amid the blue, massive, crushing void. I gulped and sobbed and, according to an eyewitness of irreproachable repute and excellent eyesight (my very close friend Norland S. Nib who, by an uncanny coincidence of the sort normally only found in the novels of Thomas Hardy, was driving by in the opposite direction at the wheel of a carnival's blue, open-mouthed brontosaurus) I could be seen limping down Regent's Park Road, apparently saying "heugh, heugh, heugh" in winded surprise. Afterwards, through the window of my haunted garret, I watched streams of testimonies run down the panes and into the gutters, making tiny screechings and a brittle whispering noise. Was that what you wanted? Brave bright murderous day sank into hideous night. Irreversible now is her snapped smile, unique the hypostatic blotches on my left calf! Know that I am still blue-eyed and lusty albeit somewhat heavier, scant of breath and slumping a bit. It is said that I give the impression of deformity without any nameable mal-formation. I cannot deny that I speak with a husky, whiskery and somewhat broken voice. I am a trifle hard-of-hearing these days, a little petulant and quirky. For some years now my clothes have been very untidy. As for my hair! I require much shampoo and frequent changes of sheet. My mind is a tireless crucible, concrete and fastidious. See – faster and faster it goes! What? Is that a blister on her brow? Ho there! Fetch me my tablets and a volume by Lenin. Undo this button. The die is cast. There is no turning back. What freezings have I felt, what dark days seen! One must try to wriggle through. I think, and speak of other things. Bring me a sparadrap and a lined refill pad with margins – preferably 297 x 210mm. Who therefore will help me staunch the sticky, salty surge of memory? Dr Ernst Philipp Barthel's spheric space theory shows beyond all doubt that the earth is the under-half of the universe! Since she left, I have never doubted it.

2

So! Some of you, I perceive, drifted in by mistake and now have to attend your scheduled lectures. Very well. I understand. Please try and leave quietly. I see others have buses and trains to catch, plane tickets to book, telephone calls to make. Others – hurry my friends! – have important letters which must not miss the last collection. Some of you who are leaving doubtless have appointments to keep with humourless irritable dentists, bluff incompetent doctors, grim unjust intimidating courts of law presided over by reactionary cretinous poltroons, opticians, fatherly recruiting officers of our armed forces, not to mention important meetings with astronomers who have a special interest in that southern hemisphere constellation introduced in 1763 by Nicolas Louis de Lacaille to commemorate the air pump invented by the physicist Robert Boyle, house-painters keen to have a chinwag about Trotsky's theory of combined and uneven development, biochemists researching the human gut, Marxist theorists bitterly divided over questions of ideology, hegemony and the state, campaigners for the rights of ped-estrians, mechanics bearing an uncanny resemblance to Dick Van Dyke in *Mary Poppins,* oily menders of bicycles, placid patchers of ruptured aerostats, macrocephalic blondes, gently throbbing lovers with paunches, shiny philatelists, gap-toothed beaming ("the tea's in the pot") aunts, burly pals and surly debtors, extraordinarily well read drunkards, aspiring astro-nauts apparelled in unusual costumes, flushed freelance journalists and bald violinists entirely ignorant, as most musicians are, of the fact that on the feast of Corpus Christi 1381 rebels from Kent and Essex crossed London Bridge unopposed and entered the city, where they were welcomed by the London poor, who had already begun to destroy the hated Duke of Lancaster's Savoy Palace in the Strand. Go. By all means go! But please remember to close the doors after you. A million thanks. Now where were we? What – So! The power-cut we had all been half-expecting. Surprising how quickly it gets dark at this time of year. Not to worry. You cannot see me and I cannot see you, but I shall soldier on regardless. I cannot see you but I sense your presence. Do you know that for a moment I thought everyone had gone and that there was no one here? Ridiculous! It's not every day you get the chance to learn about the Aleppo Button, is it? You can't fool me. O, du Geliebte meiner siebenundzwanzig Sinne, ich liebe dir! Du deiner dich dur, ich dir, du mir. – Wir? I sense your presence. I think I can hear your low breathing. Are you asleep? How well I remember that time you turned to me with your bright terminator's eyes and said, "My bounty is as boundless as the sea, my love as deep.

The more I give to thee, the more I have, for both are infinite."
I was touched and impressed. So long ago, now. Now I am old
and cold, with subdued eyes. I hear the whining and tinkling of
a hootchy kootchy show. It's an hour later in the east. I crawl
among the skin and shell of things. I will not – Only chemists
write letters! Besides, there is a painful fold in this book of
memory. I – Where was I? The button, I was going to say
something about the button. The button is a humble object,
found in the dictionary between "Buttock" (the convexity of a
ship behind, under the stern) and "Button bush" (the North
American shrub, *Cephalanthus occidentalis)*. A button is a
knob, or a small ball, or a disk of metal or some other
substance used to fasten the dress, to make a button one
requires a button-mould, which is a wooden blank over which
the material is stretched to make the button complete. The
adjective "Buttony" (having many buttons) has fallen out of
common use. I am preparing a definitive anthology entitled
The Button in World Literature. Let me whet your palate with
a few enticing morsels.

(i)   Pray you vndo this Button. Thanke you Sir.
                          Shakespeare, *King Lear*

(ii)   To the third button, he had attached a bronze
        chainlet ...
                Mikhail Lermontov (trans. Vladimir Nabokov
                    in collaboration with Dmitri Nabokov),
                                    A Hero of Our Time

(iii)   They glance nervously at their watches. None of
        them presses the "B" button.
                          Robert Coover, *The Elevator*

3

So far so good. Why? I'll tell you bloody why. Cacodaemons are
put to flight by melody because they shun the First Cause,

which is the beginning of all harmony, and of necessity they are greatly wounded by sweet music, which derives its influence from the First Cause, and so they flee from it as best they can, just as bees, moved in their airy souls to harmony, by the plangent stirring of the air, follow where harmony leads, and because when the membrane which they have inside them is sweetly struck the bees are moved, and are delighted, and, buzzing boisterously, gaily follow the pipe to the swarm, in much the same way as the essences of all things flow in disposition from the First Cause and on dissolution are called back and flow to it lest being revert to non-being, or something into nothing, as a consequence of which, as any fool could see, the swan, with a presentiment of its death, glimpses liberty, and sings by a kind of natural instinct, uttering sweet songs even as its tongue fails. Got that? Good. And so our minutes, our dark and darkening and desirable minutes, speed to their soft cinereous end. Soon it will be time to bring out the Aleppo Button and give it a good airing. So far so good. Say, honey, since there's just you and me left why don't you come back to my place and I'll show you the Aleppo Button there? It might be easier that way. I've had my fill of darkness and emptiness and chemical odours. Besides, I never liked standing on platforms. The underlying hollowness of stages is not without danger or metaphysical stress. When we are born we shriek at the prospect. I always feel queasy when faced by the drunken tilt of a lectern. We could light some candles, open a bottle of Gros Plant du Pays Nantais. You could unbutton your blouse if you felt hot. Central heating can be so stuffy, don't you find? Have I ever told you I can hum over half of Bartók? Afterwards we could listen to the shipping forecast together. Afterwards, if there is still time and I have it in me, I shall take six deep breaths and clamber up on to the roof. There I shall bellow "Some shall be pardoned, some punished!" or perhaps "There was a ship ... " or "No finger smudges! No wasted time!" or maybe "Psychoanalysis plus Marx is the science of ghosts!" or "Rejoice with the Skuttle-Fish, who foils his foe by the effusion of his ink!" or perhaps an educational 'The number of bee-hives in Bohemia in the year 1900 was 199,604!" or even a teasing "Twee bergketens lopen zo ongeveer van noord naar zuid door de republiek en vormen een aantal dalen en plateaus" or a faintly Biblical "O thou City, thou hypocritical City!" or perhaps a cautionary "Solid metallic objects of unknown origin and purpose are openly operating in our major cities!" or "Call Haunce Herkin Glukin Skellam Flapdragon!" or "The dark eagles!" or "Proust's chronology is extremely difficult to follow!" or "My raspberry's leaking!" or "The masses of the workers are capable not only of great dreams, but they have in them the power to make dreams come true!" or "Let Darda with a Leech bless the Name of the Physician of body & soul!" or "Whatever happened to Dorcas?" or "The homeland of Marxist theory remains where it has always been, the real human object, in all its manifestations!" or "Never was a story of more woe!" or "Let us be grateful for the skill and energy of Dr L. Jerabek, without – " or "My racket has gone blooey!" or "The truth is that an enormous enterprise of indoctrination is carried out in Britain, day in and day out, by a multitude of different agencies; but that the nature of this enterprise is often obscured!" or "Potatoes must not be stowed between decks or in unventilated store rooms, as they develop poisonous gases!" or "What wond'rous life is this I lead!" or "The campaigns of Genghis Khan and Tamerlane were child's play in comparison with the doings of civilised nations from 1914 to 1918" or "Tseep! Tseep! Tseep!" or "Splice the main brace!" or "Clear the ambiguities!" Then, exhilarated, I will scramble down again and get back to the business in hand. To splice the main brace (i.e. to issue an extra allowance of grog) is easily done. Clearing the ambiguities is a more challenging task. Are the differences in the earliest texts of *M. William Shak-speare: / HIS / True Chronicle Historie of the life and / death of King LEAR and his three / Daughters. With the* unfortunate life of *Edgar*, sonne / *and heire to the Earle of Gloster, and his / sullen and assumed humor of / TOM of Bedlam: /* As it was played before the Kings Maiestie at Whitehall vpon / S. Stephans night in Christmas Hollidayes.

By his Maiesties seruants playing usually at the Gloabe / on the Bancke-side. the consequence of intoxicated or tired or hurried or merely slovenly compositors, or of the careless transcription of the playwright's own autograph MS., or of the use of Shakespeare's company's prompt-book together with a revised prompt-book, or of the furtive, underhand deployment of Timothy Bright's rud-imentary system of shorthand, *Characterie,* or of a reporter's memorizing from a theatrical MS., or of a memorial reconstruction made by the entire company during a provincial tour necessitated by someone in the company having carelessly left the prompt-book (and the author's manuscript also, if the prompt-book was a transcript) in London, or of memorial reconstructions by ageing actors in the glum rain-sodden provinces months or even years after they had last performed the play? How many children had Lady Macbeth? Did Lear die believing Cordelia was still alive? Was Sir Francis Bacon (as Dodd argues) the illegitimate product of a secret liaison between Queen Elizabeth and the Earl of Leicester, who adopted the pen-name "Shake-spear" to indicate that he was the Shaker of the Spear of Knowledge at the Serpent of Ignorance and whose sonnets transmit coded messages, e.g. Sonnet XXI, which is NOT WHAT IT SEEMS but actually contains the secret communication *"Alice has a Ring: With the Worshipful Master a Worthy Sacred Symbol",* a charming gesture from Bacon to his wife? Or was J. Thomas Looney correct in *"Shakespeare" Identified* (1920) in exposing Edward De Vere, the seventeenth Earl of Oxford, as the real author, a man almost certainly acquainted with the geographical details of Verona, and probably with some knowledge of Elsinore, a man who felt he had a mission to expose what was rotten in the state of England and whose writings as "Shakspear" are NOT WHAT THEY SEEM but are in fact sardonic and mischievous portrayals of highly placed public figures who subsequently conspired to cover up De Vere's savage picture of the truth, assisted in their scandalous suppression of the true facts by the Earl's own decision to publish his work under a pseudonym in order to avoid the understandable embarrassment (for a nobleman) of being associated with the low, contemptible trade of writing, not to mention persecution? What, for that matter, has happened to the Dooms of Cnut? What are the statistical chances of being (i) abducted by aliens for a short and probably unpleasant medical investigation (ii) undergoing a spontan-eous and alas fatal combustion, while on a visit to Essex by car, using unleaded petrol and avoiding minor roads? Where is the metal hatch that leads to the underlying mechanisms of our society? What secret wheel, what hidden spring, could put in motion so wonderful an engine? Was Alek J. Hidell a Robert Louis Stevenson fan? Who remembers Bynneman, the printer? Is there really a large sullen unknown elasticated creature crouched peevishly amid the deep murk of Loch Ness? Charlie Foxtrot Tango, come in please. Are you reading me, over? Will I ever see you again? Where is my judgement fled? Is anyone there or have you all gone? Is that a whisper in the darkness or a mocking echo? Who will join me in a round-table discussion of the Aleppo Button?

4

So far so good. So, you want to know how I feel? Sore. I was sore that afternoon you lied to me, sore the day you left me. *Carajo basta de sufrir!* I was sore from sleeping on the floor. "Oh lift me as a wave, a leaf, a cloud!" I wanted to shout (although I was careful not to). I was sore from placing my buttocks, day after day, on that same empty patch of the Heath, where I pondered the ponds and the past. All that summer I was bothered by flies and decay, heartburn and moths, sunburn and emptiness. All that autumn, under a hot and copper sky, I waited for the first icicles. Winter came, coldly exaggerating the emptiness of the sky, the emptiness of the room, the emptiness of the bed. There were no icicles. My mouth was dry, my throat was sore. I woke each morning from uneasy dreams. Are you listening? Set you down this. The Aleppo Button – sometimes known as the Baghdad Boil or the

Delhi Sore, according to the places where it is commonly found – begins as a pinprick pimple. It spreads and turns into an ulcer. It often leaves unsightly scars. It is caused by the bite of a sand-fly. One attack of the Aleppo Button usually gives lifelong protection against any subsequent attack. See – there is my scar, and there another. Farewell, my Jumbly Girl, my Odradek, my little button. Time to be off to my position at the Workers' Accident Insurance Institute. Dear Diary: It seems to be DARK all the time. So touched ... So touched by her presence. No date, the day doesn't have one. Am I corroded by the excesses of individualism and aesthetic caprice? Fleet Street, 13 September 1819: Knowing well that my life must be passed in fatigue and trouble, I have been endeavouring, I have been endeavouring, I have been endeavouring ... No use. This morning I scarcely know what I am doing. All I know is that my love is as a fever, my thoughts and discourse as – I am going to – I hope all will be well. We must be patient. And so to end, to sleep, to die, so to speak. All so long ago. We'll go no more a roving. Perhaps after tomorrow – But no. Never. Life has a varying offensive. What did I expect from it – full coverage against all possible risks? So long ... Soft now. The wind comes from the sky. A last word or two before I go. The general contradictions of revolution are always difficult for art, which seeks perfected forms. The butt-end is the larger end of a spar. A spar (which you will find in your dictionary between "Span-Worm" – the larva of a looper-moth or a canker-worm – and "Sparadrap" – a cloth smeared with wax) is a long piece of timber or a general term for masts, yards, gaffs and booms. Epictetus is in some ways my favourite philosopher. Please forgive me for carrying on in this way. Fifteen years underground, after all! O Christ, that ever this should be! Will it never have done? So long the empty years, the burning empty summers, the desolating winters, so long the empty hours of the night, the darkness. So late. So soon the time to say so long, the end. So? So far to go, so little time left. So much left – What else did you expect? So let me say what happens next. Simple. The end.

5

So. The end? Not so. Succedit musica larvis. To make an end is
– *Drum afar off* – to make a beginning. Never an ending,
always echoes, shadows, traces, ashes and sparks, sounds of a
strange kind, cracked bells, dull remote reverberations,
tickings, faint distant hissings as of snakes in the grass or rain
beating on the window of a garret three floors up in York or the
slow death of a punctured aerostat, a clamorous ringing in my
ears as of Austrian cowbells, a tintinnabulation turning to an
archaic telephone tinkle, washed-out horns, whisperings, dull
glimmerings, an afterglow, dust in the air suspended. The wind
blowing across the dimes, the shingle, the Heath, the grasses.
O, wert thou in the cauld blast ... In my ears the greedy time-
devouring roar of that glaucous-grey polluted ocean which has
rocked sickenly unendingly between us sin' auld lang syne. No,
I haven't the strength to endure it any longer. Let this my right
hand crawl crab-like over the clean white page for the last
time. Time for your poor whirl-brain to lie down now among
the pebbles with the other old worn-out things, lie down now
in the gust, the whirlwind, and the flaw of rain and hailstones.
Time to snuggle up to the jetsam, the cuttlefish shells, the old
bits of stick, the earth's dark veins, the warmth of worms and
slumber. Soonest mended, that's what they say, so long. So
long, have to dash. No use now getting off at Bethnal Green
and making enquiries at the Universal Button Co. No use
bringing me that submarine or the map of Syria. I am engulfed
in a deep valley of mist. I am pooped and listing furiously.
Harsh cries of shearwaters, I am whirling round and round.
Dark shadows cast by ceiling lights swing in the alleyways,
dark shadows foil across ladders and ventilators, the confined
space of cabins, the gaffe and booms. Too late now for your
poor tired tesselist to complete his 800-page semi-
autobiographical novel, *The Ramifications*. Too late now to
build that rocket and propel myself into space in hope of
making a new life on Azuria or Genesistrine or some other
hypothetical vast Fortean superconstruction elegantly adrift in

silent sparkling space and crammed with intriguing rubbish including a bucket of toads and a heap of writhing mackerel. Altogether too late. So short the days now, dead of winter and short of breath, going fast. Four in the morning, end of December. The night wind whispers in my ear. Spurt of Radio One from somebody's kitchen. This Wheel's on Fire and – So long, now. So short now, my span. So brittle my bones. A daily spoonful of cod liver oil works wonders but in my condition is alas of limited efficacy. Skin tight as rubber here, slack as anything there, flesh crumbling like a Munich pastry, crumbling like the cliffs where once we climbed up the steps to the white lighthouse long ago, the gulls squealing and shrieking and – You would not recognise me now with my paper crown, my flippers, my sad red nose. Little left to say, too much unsaid. A born Lear. There is no end but addition. Come here, go hence. Somewhat dishevelled and out of shape I seem to see a compact, hour-glass-waisted figure getting smaller and smaller and further and further away from me ... *Ah, Der Wasserfall, la soledad, la lluvia, los caminos* ... The moon shines in my face. Ceaselessly, unreasonably grieving, my future ease must depend upon forgetfulness. Nobody here now. All gone. Just me and the jars and that worried-looking embalmed foetus ... Open wounds, size of a pinprick. Christ, what a stink! What? Still here? Such stamina! I hope you made notes, I hope you understood. Please draw your breath, switch on your torch and leave me now. I am quite spent with thought. On second thoughts, stick around if you want to. Watch me rot and shrink. Remembering that bodies do not inevitably decompose but do so only within a relatively narrow temperature-range gives me the shivers. Cold water over my head! My head is burning, everything is spinning round and round. The weather is against me. The wind and rain will take care of the ashes. On top of that hill there, on the other side of the river. I must show you. I – No. No time, now. So long! I shall not vanish from your sight but turn, bit by bit, to calcium and phosphorus. Maybe a storm will get up, whirling my drifting dust in your direction. May it tickle your nose and make you sneeze! May it infiltrate your buttonholes and make you want to scratch. May it cause you to wonder, just a little, about – *Drum afar off* – the Aleppo Button.

Afterwords

Who, I wonder, now remembers the occasion when the protagonist of "The Shrinking of Theever" really *did* fire a 105mm shell at Pleasant Island? The sway of the camera, the all-too-familiar to and fro of insipid question and bland answer, the rocking motion of the waves, all blurred together to produce a sudden powerful sense of nausea and in the dim glow of the television I could see my hand reaching out eagerly for pencil and paper ... Years later I saw that impressive film *The Terminator* and everything clicked into place. Certain minor details in this story have been taken from Frederick Cowles's "Princess of Darkness", published for the first time in Richard Dalby's fine anthology, *Dracula's Brood* (1987).

Dobson's comments about the *Titanic* are taken from Paul O'Flinn's *Them and Us in Literature* (1975), while the most important word in "Dead Paraguayans" derives from Augusto Roa Bastos's essay, "Writing: a Metaphor of Exile", in John King's critical anthology, *Modern Latin American Writing* (1987), which I first read long after writing this story.

"Dodd" in "The Aleppo Button" refers to Alfred Dodd's *The Personal Poems of Francis Bacon (Our Shake-speare) The Son of Queen Elizabeth* (1937); information about Bohemian bee-hives is taken from the authoritative *Guide to the Royal City of Prague and to the Kingdom of Bohemia* (Prague, 1906). M. Alphonse Ratisbonne, mentioned in "Tinctures, Stains, Relics", will be found in the index of William James's *The Varieties of Religious Experience*.

On one of my bookshelves, wedged tightly between a crumbling fifty-cent copy of *Lo!* and a handsome hardback edition of *The Dragon and the Disc*, is a battered Sphere paperback by John A. Keel. On the cover an empty road cuts between a deserted gas station and a windowless barn. From the out-of-focus cirrus which streaks the yellow featureless sky looms a grotesque humanoid figure with a lipless skull-toothed mouth, indecipherable eyes and an improbably webbed scalp. For one of my stories I have, of course, borrowed the title of Keel's book – *Strange Creatures from Time and Space*. I do not think I shall ever give it back.

Ellis Sharp, London, January 1991

Afterthoughts

In the late nineteen-eighties I was introduced to Paul Byrne, who with his friend Max Décharné had in 1986 set up Malice Aforethought Press. Based in Walthamstow, in East London, this small press dedicated itself to eccentric comic fiction, often with a satirical bent. I discovered that Paul and I had common political and cultural tastes and in due course, after various drinking sessions at The Rose and Crown on Hoe Street, I was encouraged to contribute some writing of my own. This expanded version of *The Aleppo Button* emerged from that heady period. It now includes the first story I wrote, "General Jaruzelski's Sunglasses", together with four other short pieces written around this time: "The Problem with the President's Mouth", "Dear Blank", "A Quiet Morning for the Pound" and "Giacinta's Clams". The original dedication to *The Aleppo Button*, which has been retained for this expanded edition, refers to Paul and his wife (sadly, their marriage did not endure and at some point after I had lost contact with them they divorced).

The Aleppo Button emerged from this first delirium of inspiration as a volume of satire, written in the dark shadows of the Thatcher government, howling against the state of things. Much of it, in first draft, was written at speed on my first computer – a clunky £20,000 monster which had been passed on to me by a friend working for a business which was updating its IT system. This bulky machine required a 5¼-inch floppy disk to boot it up every time it was switched on. Another disk was then inserted, which provided capacity for about a hundred pages of text. On the screen this text appeared green, in a manner reminiscent of *The Matrix*. The internet as we know it today did not exist. Text on a screen was attractive; it made revisions and additions so much easier than fiction hammered out on my Olympia typewriter, which involved ribbons, Tipp-Ex and carbon paper. The speed of composition was also influenced by the material conditions of my life at that time, which permitted only short, fragmentary periods for writing.

Looking back at this assemblage of material after thirty years I am struck by a central continuity with my later work – political satire and critique – and by a major difference. These stories possessed a wild, comic exuberance which favoured a surrealist loosening of the cage of narrative realism. Quite where this latter impulse came from I am uncertain and in time the exuberance and the anarchic imagination began to slacken and fade. The years went by. I lost touch with Max first. He moved away, pursuing his own career in music and writing. My association with Paul, who adopted the pseudonym "Frank Key", ended in 1998. After that he continued to write his own very distinctive self-illustrated tales of whimsy and nonsense, as well as developing a fan-base as a broadcaster for Resonance FM. I last saw him towards the end of the twentieth century, in the distance on a busy London street, a thin, tall figure wearing his distinctive round glasses. Paul seemed to tower above those around him. He didn't see me and soon vanished into the crowd. I never saw or spoke to him again. He died, shockingly and unexpectedly, in 2019.

Other ghosts haunt this volume. The monstrous vampire of "The Shrinking of Theever" is, of course, Margaret Thatcher, and the President of "Backyard" is Ronald Reagan. Diana, Princess of Wales, also joins these spectres. At the time when "Hitler and the Aerostat" was written she was a gigantic figure in British life, whose every action was recorded, amplified and worshipped by the corporate media. The only other fiction writer who dared to mock her in her lifetime was, I believe, J. G. Ballard.

There was also one satirical prophecy which ultimately proved remarkably accurate. "The Bloating of Nellcock", a savage comic assault on the man who was then Leader of the Labour Party, Neil Kinnock (whose persona in those days was that of a fiery and passionate Welsh radical), imagined him full of hot air, expanding in size and, plump and airborne, flapping his arms vigorously at the sight of the distant House of Lords. Sure enough Kinnock, who in 1979 had marched alongside Socialist Workers Party members at the funeral procession of Blair Peach, duly followed the trajectory of so many fizzing, hot-air Labour Party left-wingers, slithering home to the House of the Living Dead in 2005, dressed in class-traitor's robes and adopting the title Baron Kinnock. Perhaps "The Mould" is also prophetic – at any rate, from the perspective of 2021 it seems imbued with the faint intuition of a far-reaching pandemic.

The contents of *The Aleppo Button* may have been a little ahead of their time in other ways. In 2016 a popular British novelist was widely praised for his originality and ingenuity in writing a novel set entirely inside a womb and narrated from the perspective of a foetus. This marvel might seem less remarkable to anyone who has left the gleaming thoroughfares of corporate publishing and dipped their toes in those gutters of contemporary fiction which can still be found trickling through that bad, dark, dangerous district at the edge of town.

Ellis Sharp, April 2021